EMVILLE CONFIDENTIAL

EMVILLE CONFIDENTIAL

DON TREMBATH

ORCA BOOK PUBLISHERS

Library and Archives Canada Cataloguing in Publication

Trembath, Don, 1963-
Emville confidential / written by Don Trembath.

ISBN 978-1-55143-671-5

I. Title.

PS8589.R392E48 2007   jC813'.54   C2007-902770-9

First published in the United States, 2007

Library of Congress Control Number: 2007927583

Summary: Baron dreams of being like his favorite hard-boiled detectives: tough,
sexy and in control, but the reality is something quite different.

**The author would like to acknowledge
the generous financial support of the
Alberta Foundation for the Arts.**

Orca Book Publishers gratefully acknowledges the support for its publishing programs
provided by the following agencies: the Government of Canada through the Book
Publishing Industry Development Program and the Canada Council for the Arts,
and the Province of British Columbia through the BC Arts Council
and the Book Publishing Tax Credit.

Cover and text design: Teresa Bubela
Cover artwork by Gary Alphonso

ORCA BOOK PUBLISHERS
PO Box 5626, STN. B
VICTORIA, BC CANADA
V8R 6S4

ORCA BOOK PUBLISHERS
PO Box 468
CUSTER, WA USA
98240-0468

www.orcabook.com
Printed and bound in Canada.
Printed on 100% PCW paper.
10 09 08 07 • 4 3 2 1

To Bebe, my curly-haired, freckle-nosed eight-year-old, whose imagination and zest for life surpasses anything I've ever done; and to my friends Joe and Gail, for inspiring chapter one.

CHAPTER ONE

It was a long day.

A long hot day.

A long hot day in May.

Baron Colfax leaned his chair back against a wall in the shack he called his office and wiped the sweat off his forehead with the back of his hand. His partner, Myles Monahan, would be arriving soon. They had a client coming at four. A woman. At least Baron liked to think of her as a woman as he sat by himself and waited. In reality she was twelve years old, the same age as him and Myles. He wiped his forehead again, shifted a toothpick from one side of his mouth to the other and closed his eyes.

A woman appeared in the doorway. She was distraught and strikingly beautiful. Her hair was long and blond. Her clothes were stylish, expensive and clung to her curves like a Porsche 911 weaving down a mountain road.

She sat down with a quick polite smile and fiddled with her handbag. She looked as if she was trying to decide whether to leave it on her lap or put it on the floor by her chair. Her hands shook as she tried to make her decision. Lap or floor? The heat made her smooth white forehead bead with perspiration. Lap or floor?

Baron remained calm and detached as he watched her. He knew from experience that when people were stressed, even the simplest decisions could be difficult.

Her top lip started to tremble.

He offered her his pack of Camels.

"Cigarette?"

In reality, Baron had never smoked a cigarette in his life and he likely never would. Not after seeing the way his Grandma Carson suffered before she died of lung cancer. But in his daydreams — well, the detectives in all of his favorite hard-boiled detective novels smoked, and that was that.

In his dream, the woman gratefully accepted his offer. Baron thumbed his lighter. She inhaled deeply and closed her eyes. The smoke blew out through her nose and mouth and appeared to take her anxiety along with it: The handbag slipped from her lap and landed neatly on the floor by her chair.

"Thank you," she said, taking note for the first time of his muscular forearms and cool knowing eyes.

"My pleasure," he replied, lighting a cigarette of his own and blowing a thin line of smoke into the air. "My pleasure" was a line that Baron would never use in real life, except maybe if he was joking. It was too stiff and formal.

Too grown-up. In the dream, however, it was the coolest thing he could think of saying. In his dreams, Baron was always very cool. Such romantic notions of detective work frequently found their way into Baron's mind. He was famous at his school for daydreaming.

He was also epileptic, so sometimes what looked like daydreaming was actually an absence seizure. But few of his teachers ever bothered to figure out the difference, and no matter what it was that had taken his mind off his lessons, the results were always the same: His grades at school were the pits.

The woman in his dream was offering up a challenge of a different kind. She crossed her legs and settled comfortably into her chair. "You certainly know how to make a woman feel welcome," she said.

"It's better for business that way."

"My name is Veronica Knox. My friends call me Ronnie."

"My name's Baron. My friends call me for things they can't handle on their own."

She smiled. "Does that make me your friend?"

"I'll let you know."

"You like to play it cool, don't you, Baron?"

"It comes natural."

Veronica straightened herself in her chair and took another drag on her cigarette. "Well, whatever it is and whoever you are, I hope you can help me. I'm at the end of my rope here. I tried the police first. They did nothing.

I tried doing something on my own, but I failed miserably. If this doesn't work, I don't know what I'll do."

"So spill it. What's your story?"

The worry lines immediately returned to Veronica's face. "I've come for my sister."

"Look around. She's not here."

"Please. This is serious. My sister is in real trouble. I've come to ask for help on her behalf."

Baron sat in silence.

"She's been kidnapped."

"Uh-huh."

"Actually, no. She hasn't been kidnapped. She's been brainwashed by her punk boyfriend into believing that swindling money from my father is a perfectly acceptable thing to do." Giant tears began to slowly roll down Veronica's cheeks. "Patricia's so young. She's so naïve. She's even more beautiful than I am." Veronica picked up her handbag from the floor and pulled out a Kleenex. She dabbed her eyes and blew her nose. "I've tried talking to her, but she won't listen to me. She wants nothing to do with me anymore, and it's all because of him. When we were young, we were best friends. We did everything together. Now I call her on the phone, and she won't even pick up. I have to know what she's up to. For her own good."

"How much does your father know about this?"

"Nothing. He's an old man. His mind's half gone. He'd give her the shirt off his back if she asked for it."

"Has she?"

"Not yet. But she will."

"What about your mother?"

Instantly, Veronica's eyes turned to ice. The tears stopped flowing. Her lips turned white. "My stepmother, you mean? My young gorgeous stepmother? She's in on this. I know she is. She's the puppet master to that idiot my sister hooked up with. She wants my father's money more than anything else in the world."

"And you don't?"

Veronica stared for a moment before answering. "I beg your pardon?"

"I'm just wondering what makes you so different from everyone else in your family. They all seem to know what money is and what it can do. What part of it don't you understand?"

Veronica raised the cigarette to her lips, drew in, blew out, dropped what remained of it on the floor and mashed it out with the heel of her shoe. For not one second did she take her eyes off the detective before her. "So is this the way you operate? Treat everyone involved in a case as a suspect? Even the one who comes to you for help?"

"If two plus two plus two don't add up to six, that's exactly what I do."

"Is that why it's so quiet around here? You chase everyone away?"

"It's quiet here 'cause I want it quiet. It's hot 'cause Mother Nature wants it hot. Now why don't you tell me what you want and maybe we can get somewhere."

"I just told you what I want — to help my sister."

"That's not what I heard."

"Oh no?"

"Not at all."

"Why don't you tell me what you heard then?"

"I heard you say you want your old man's money protected from the vultures who want it as badly as you do. I heard you say you want me to tail your sister and her boyfriend so you can keep tabs on them while you hound-dog Mommie Dearest. I heard you say there's about as much love in your family as there is fine furniture in this office. I heard you say that you're the only one who can be trusted, and that if something were to accidentally happen to your old man, the last person responsible would be you. I don't believe a word of it. Is that enough, or should I go on?"

"That's enough."

"Then get up and leave or get on with it."

"Are you always this direct with people?"

"Only when I'm in a good mood."

"It's very becoming, you know." She arched one of her eyebrows.

"Oh, really?"

"Oh yes. You're becoming more appealing to me every time you open your mouth." She smiled. "I love a man who knows he's a man."

"As opposed to...?"

She giggled. "You're funny too. I love to laugh. It relaxes me."

"I could put you to sleep with my George Bush imitation."

"I think I'd enjoy that."

"But with all this laughing going on, how would we keep track of who's doing what with Papa Bear's dough?"

"We'd find a way, somehow, I'm sure."

"I'm not."

"Oh, come on. You're so good at what you do."

"What I do is weed out the real from the unreal, the fairy queens from the princesses, the sad people from the attention-grabbers."

"Where am I in all that?"

"I'm not sure yet, but it ain't lookin' good, especially if you like to laugh so much. I don't like people who laugh all the time. They either got something to hide or they can't remember where they hid it."

Without flinching, Veronica scooped up her handbag and rose to her feet. Baron watched her all the way up. Even he had to admit she was a cool drink of water on such a scalding hot day.

"They told me you were tough," she said. "They didn't say anything about making false accusations that were way out of line. Maybe you're not my kind of man after all."

"I have two arms and two legs. I bet that's enough to qualify me right there."

She gave him a snotty look as she walked out the door.

"Dream on, little man. I'll let you know how it works out."

"I'll read about it in the papers first."

The door banged shut after she left.

Baron's eyes jerked open. His chair thumped to the floor.

His partner, Myles, was standing in the doorway.

CHAPTER TWO

"You still chewing those stupid toothpicks?" Myles said. He was slightly taller than Baron, and heavier by a few pounds. He had a thick untamed pile of dark curly hair and he wore glasses.

"They're good," said Baron, straightening himself on his chair. "This one was chocolate." He removed the toothpick from his mouth and flipped it into the small garbage can by the door. The daydream lingered in his mind, but only for a moment — he was very good at switching back and forth from his dreamworld to reality. He ran his fingers through his side-parted brown hair.

The two boys had been friends since they were five years old.

They lived in the quiet rural town of Emville, Alberta. Baron had four siblings — three older, one younger; Myles was an only child. They each had a full set of parents.

The office was in the far back corner of Baron's back-yard. It was twelve feet square, with a small porch outside the front door and a window box filled with flowers hanging under the small west-facing window. The window box bothered Myles to no end. "What are we, a green-house or a detective agency?" he said. The particleboard on the outside was painted to match the chocolate-colored shingles on the roof. The style inside was rustic, at best. There was no electricity and just the one window, which looked almost directly into the garage. Light was allowed in by keeping the door wide open, a problem in the summer when the mosquitoes arrived. (The agency moved inside the Colfax home during the winter.) The walls were finished with drywall and leftover beige paint.

Myles dropped his backpack against the back wall of their office and lifted a folding chair down from a hook on the wall.

"You may as well get one down for her too," said Baron, referring to the client they were expecting.

Myles lifted down a second chair. "Who is she, anyway?"

"I have no idea."

"Why is she coming here?"

"I don't know."

"How'd she hear about us?"

"No clue."

"Who took the call?"

"She left a message."

"That's weird," said Myles.

Baron shrugged his shoulders. To him, a mysterious phone call from a mysterious female was part of the territory of being a detective. Part of the romance. The intrigue. "Why is that weird?"

"She's hiding something," said Myles, who had not one drop of romantic blood in his body. "I can tell you that right now. She's going to be a client and a suspect all rolled into one. Just watch."

"We'll see," said Baron.

"I know we'll see," said Myles. "I just told you that."

Thanks to his parents, Gus and Moira, Myles was suspicious by nature. As a family, they were well known in the town of Emville for their combative and opinionated ways. They ran a coffee shop called In Yer Mug! on Main Street, right next to the Helping Hand Store. Gus, a retired military man, also wrote a straight-talking column for the *Emville Reflector*, the local weekly newspaper. Once called "The Cynical Side of Things," the column was now simply called, "Hey, Monahan!" after the way people in town addressed him.

Myles himself was no stranger to self-expression and the pitfalls that occasionally came with it. He enjoyed writing and often checked his dad's columns before they went off to the presses. He also liked to sit in on the frank discussions and rousing arguments that took place among the regulars at the coffee shop. He had recently begun raising concerns of his own at school on such topical issues as healthcare, education and tax reform.

His teachers appreciated his efforts. Many of them said he was a natural for student council, if he could ever get anyone to vote for him. Privately, they all agreed that he was a bit too much like his father for his own good.

The client arrived punctually at four o'clock. She was taller than both boys and blond. Her skin was smooth and lightly tanned.

The boys offered her a seat; they sat back in their chairs, crossed their arms and pursed their lips. They looked as if they were performing a choreographed routine, which in a way they were.

"I'm here about a blue whale," she said. "I want you to find it...for my sister."

"Approximately when did she lose it?" said Baron.

She shook her head. "I don't know exactly." She sniffed into a Kleenex. "I can't remember."

Baron nodded understandingly.

Beside him, Myles sprang from his chair and grabbed his backpack. He brought it over to his chair, sat down and started to search through it. "We should be writing this down," he said in a half-whisper.

Baron agreed. "You write. I'll ask the questions."

Myles stopped his search. "Why should I write? I wrote the last time."

Baron waited before answering. He did not want to appear distracted in front of their client.

"You write two times, then I write two times."

"Since when?"

"Since always."

Myles grew more agitated. "It hasn't always been like that. We alternate. You, then me. You, then me. You, then me. You —"

"I get it." Baron smiled politely at their client, and then turned his full attention to his partner. "Okay, I'll write, then you write. Grab me the notepad."

Myles's eyes widened. "*Hello*. That's what I'm trying to do. I can't find it."

Baron frowned. "What do you mean you can't find it?"

"I mean exactly what I just said. I can't find it."

"Well, where is it?"

"How am I supposed to know? What am I, your mother? I thought I put it in here."

Baron smiled again at the girl, who was picking up her own backpack and reaching into it. She pulled out a small writing pad with a tiny pencil attached to it. "Would you like to use this?" She passed it across the small, round, wooden table that stood unevenly on the floor between them.

Baron hesitated. It did not look professional to use a client's notepad and pencil.

"Take it," said Myles. "We've got nothing else. I must have left ours in my bedroom."

Baron reluctantly reached for the pad and pencil. "Thank you. I'm sorry about this. I'll make sure we have our own supplies the next time we get together."

The girl continued to sniffle. "It's okay. As long as you help my sister."

Baron snapped open the pad and resumed the interrogation. "So you can't tell us when she lost it — is that correct?"

"Not exactly, no."

"When did you find out she lost it?"

The girl thought for a moment. "About a year ago."

Baron stopped writing and raised his head. "A *year* ago?"

"Uh-huh."

"And you're only starting to look for it now?"

"Yes."

"May I ask why?"

"Because I'd like to find it for her."

"No, I mean, why now if she lost it a year ago?"

The girl sighed deeply. Her shoulders sagged, and for a moment she closed her eyes as if to collect herself. "It's a long story. I'd really rather not go into it at the moment."

Baron hesitated; then he wrote more notes in his pad.

In his mind he pretended to be the hard-boiled detective that he was in his dreams. We've all got secrets, kid, he said to himself. You keep yours and I'll keep mine. It's less complicated that way.

"What school does she go to?" Myles stepped into the interview.

"She doesn't go to school," said the girl.

"She already graduated?"

"Not quite."

"She quit?"

"She left. That's all you need to know."

"Usually we're the ones who decide that."

"Not this time."

Myles studied the girl closely as she answered his questions. "Are you close to your sister?"

She nodded. "Yes, we're like this." She held up two fingers and crossed them over each other.

"So you do things together?"

"Of course."

"Like what?"

"Like everything. We're sisters. She's with me all the time."

Baron caught up with his notes; then he gave her another look. He hadn't noticed the dash of freckles across her nose or the deep blue of her eyes before.

"Describe this whale to me, if you don't mind," he said. "Was it big? Small? A piece of jewelry? An inflatable toy?"

"I don't know how to explain it." She lowered her eyes to the floor as she answered.

"Excuse me?"

She took another Kleenex out of her pocket and blew her nose. "I don't know what it looked like. I never actually saw it. I just know that she lost it, and she wants it back."

The two boys stared at the girl, glanced at each other and then looked back again at the girl.

"You don't know what it looks like?" said Baron.

"Not really, no. I don't."

"You have no idea?" said Myles.

"Nope."

"So you want us to find something even though we don't know what it looks like?" said Baron.

"For ten dollars," the girl said, recovering her composure. "Five now, five after you've found it."

She told them her name was Sharla. Her sister was Carla. Their mother was Marla. Their father, according to Sharla, had been kicked out of the house three years ago.

"He wasn't nice," was all she said about him.

Sharla went to Easton Middle School, which explained why the boys had never seen her before — they both went to Emville Junior High.

She left on her bicycle.

The boys watched her ride down the street; then they returned to their office. It was 4:30 on Wednesday afternoon. She would be returning Saturday at 2:00 PM for an update.

"We don't have a lot of time," said Baron.

"We don't have a lot of anything," said Myles. "We have no clues, no leads, no useful information of any kind. We have a request to find something, and we don't even know what it looks like."

"My guess is that whatever we're looking for looks something like a blue whale," said Baron, sitting in his chair.

"You think?" Myles preferred to remain standing.

"Yes, I do."

"Well, let's go find it then."

"After you."

Neither boy moved. Baron leaned back in his chair and stretched. Myles shifted his weight from one foot to the other and started to think. His world was different than Baron's, mostly due to his parents. Gus Monahan was a man who'd seen it all, and what he hadn't seen, he'd heard about from Moira. Everything in Gus's life was either black or white, good or bad, right or wrong. There were no in-betweens, no shortcuts and no free rides. Dead was dead, alive was alive, and as long as you could tell one from the other you would be okay. Myles loved to listen to his father and he admired him greatly. His mother, on the other hand, could drive him crazy.

"You know what Gus would say?" he said. Myles was the only boy Baron knew who called his parents by their first names.

"What?"

"He'd say she's lying."

Baron nodded. That is what Gus would say. "About what?"

"I'm not sure. About the fact that a blue whale is missing, or that it ever existed, or that it belonged to her sister, or that she even has a sister."

Baron continued to nod. Then he had a seizure.

Myles caught him by the shoulder before he could fall off the chair and held him there for the few seconds that the seizure lasted.

"You okay?" Myles said, when he could see in his partner's eyes that the seizure was over.

"Uh-huh. Yup." Baron straightened himself. He did not have the kind of seizures that frightened people because they appeared so destructive. His seizures were quicker and much less disturbing to witness, but equally troublesome for him. On some days he had ten of them; on others he could have fifty or more. One day at school three years ago, he'd had a seizure and peed himself — a humiliation that many of his classmates had never allowed him to forget.

The medication he'd first been prescribed had made him tired all the time. When it was changed, he became dizzy, weak and unable to keep his food down. He was currently being treated by a homeopath who'd been recommended to his mother by a family friend. The remedies he was on had reduced the number of seizures he had, but had not eliminated them completely.

"You were saying?" Baron said.

"What part did you miss?" asked Myles.

"I don't know. The last thing I heard was 'She's lying.'"

Myles repeated his theory that everything the girl said could be called into question. "That's what Gus would say, anyway," he concluded.

"Okay," said Baron, getting up to speed. "But remember, you're not Gus. So just because he thinks she's lying doesn't mean you have to."

"I know that. But listen to her. What kind of a story was that? 'My sister lost a blue whale two stinkin' years ago.

I don't know what it looks like. I don't know where she was when she lost it, even though we do everything together because we're so very close. Can you find it for me please? I'll pay you for it.' Does that not sound a bit weird to you? I mean, if it's so important, why isn't her sister here asking us to find it? Answer me that one before we go anywhere else with this."

Baron had to admit that Myles had a point, but there were still flaws in his argument.

"But why did she come see us at all then, if she's lying about everything?"

"I don't know."

"How do we find out?"

Myles thought for a moment. As a new idea came to him, he snapped his fingers. "We go to her school and confront her. We take the offensive. We say, 'Honey, tell us straight up what you're up to, or hire some other suckers to find your whale, if there even is one, which we doubt.'"

Baron had expected something like this. "'Take the offensive'" was a motto that Myles had been raised on. "And if she proves to us that it's all true?"

Myles shook his head. "Won't happen. As sure as this day is twenty-four hours long, I know she's lying."

"Those tears she was crying seemed pretty real."

"So she's a psycho. She can make herself cry on command. I don't know."

"What if she is a psycho? She comes at us with something, what are we gonna do?"

"You know that won't be a problem," said Myles, puffing out his chest.

Baron rolled his eyes and shook his head.

"Can you think of a better idea?" asked Myles.

"Not really."

"Let's go with mine then, so we don't waste any more of our time."

With reluctance, Baron agreed. "All right, we go to her school and find out what's going on."

"Tomorrow," said Myles, putting the final touches on his plan. "Three o'clock sharp. I'll meet you at the bike racks."

"Tomorrow," confirmed Baron. Then he had another seizure.

CHAPTER THREE

The next day after school, Baron and Myles met at the bike racks and began walking to Easton Middle School, which sat directly across a large playing field from Emville Junior High. It was a warm afternoon. Kids swarmed around the schoolyard — playing, running, clambering to get on their buses, riding their bikes. The two boys moved through the crowds without interruption. No one called for them to wait up or asked where they were going. Kerry Tucker, a big kid who played hockey with fourteen-year-olds, called out, "Hey Baron, you pee your pants again?"

Baron ignored him and kept walking.

Beside him, Myles expressed his enthusiasm for the encounter that awaited them. "I love it when we catch a con." He pumped his fist in the air. "She thought she was so good, telling us her sappy little story. I had her figured out in two seconds. Two seconds was all I needed to figure her out."

Like his mother, Myles tended to repeat himself, especially when he was excited.

"How long?" said Baron.

"Two seconds. She's probably waiting for her school bus right now, staring off into the distance, wondering what those two little no-brains she hired are doing. She probably thinks we're going through people's garbage to see if her whale got thrown out somewhere."

They were almost at her school. Myles had just opened his mouth to say something more when he was interrupted by the *brrrring! brrrring!* of a bicycle bell, followed by a voice calling out behind them, "Hey, guys, wait up."

The two boys stopped and turned around.

"Sorry I'm late. I meant to meet you at the bike racks at three, but my stupid tires needed air. I think I have a slow leak in both of them, if that's possible."

It was Sharla. She was wearing light blue shorts and a white T-shirt. Her long wavy hair flowed freely from beneath her bike helmet. She came to a stop and smiled at them. "You guys walk fast. Man, I had to really race across that field to catch up with you."

She was in much better spirits than she had been the day before. There were no tears streaming down her face or signs of sadness in her eyes.

"Saved you a few steps, anyway." She motioned toward the school. "So, you wanna just stand here and talk or go someplace else? Doesn't really matter to me — I have my bike. There's a 7-Eleven just over there, if you want a slush.

You guys probably know that already, though, don't you? I keep forgetting you've lived here a lot longer than I have. I just moved here three months ago."

Neither boy said anything.

"You're probably wondering what I'm doing here, right? Well, after riding away from your house yesterday, I doubled back down the alleyway and snuck up behind your little shed-thingy and listened to you. Pretty good, eh? I can be very sneaky when I want to be." She turned her attention to Myles. "You don't like me very much, do you? Bummer. I know who your dad is, by the way. Eww. I read his column once — not my favorite food, if you know what I mean. Every time I see his face in that little newspaper he writes for, I cover it up and throw it in the recycling bin."

Upon hearing her views on his father, Myles narrowed his eyes in anger.

Sharla took notice. "Don't make that face at me. You look just like him when you do that."

Baron was still too shocked to speak. Never, neither in real life nor in his daydreams, had he ever been so surprised by the development in a case.

Myles, on the other hand, was preparing for battle. "I am a green belt in karate," he said, speaking very deliberately through clenched teeth. "I have always been told never to use what I have learned unless it was absolutely necessary. I believe that time has come. Oi!" He sprang into a lethal fighting position, his hands held stiffly in front of his face, his eyes smoldering with intensity.

"You insult Gus, you insult me. Now you pay."

"What about your glasses?" said Sharla, still straddling her bicycle.

"You won't get close enough to my face for them to matter." Myles slowly began to inch forward.

"Oh no?"

"Not a chance."

"What karate school do you go to?"

"I am a member of the Gordo School of Karate, second year."

"Oh yeah? I've just joined the Moran School. I'm going to be a junior instructor next month. I'm a brown belt, fourth year. Oi! that in your breakfast."

Myles stopped moving and lowered his hands.

"What, you never heard that expression before?" Sharla said. "I always say that. Not the *Oi!* part. It's supposed to be 'Put that in your breakfast.' I just thought I'd jazz it up for you, since you like the word *Oi!* so much. You said it with such intensity."

A quizzical look replaced the anger on Myles's face. "Who are you?"

"You mean for real? My name is Rebecca Alyson Amanda Stephanie Wilson. I'm twelve years old. I'm home-schooled by my tired, way-too-controlling mother, Joanne. I moved to your beautiful little town three months ago from Winnipeg, where I lived for four years after moving from Nova Scotia. We used to move around a lot, as you can probably tell. My mom and dad are no longer together, which is kind of a downer, but at least they don't fight anymore. We live with my Auntie Heather now. She thinks my mom is crazy for teaching me at home, which I happen to agree with. It's the only thing my auntie and I agree on, by the way. She really ripples my chips, if you want to know the truth, but seeing as how you two are such fine private detectives, I'm sure you knew that already. Anything else you want to know? Do I really have a sister? No, I don't. Did she ever have a blue whale? Obviously not. If I don't have a sister, how could she have a blue whale? Are you following all this or would you like to write it down? I didn't bring my backpack with me, so I don't have another pencil and pad to give you. I'd like them back, by the way. That was not part of the act. I was just covering up your incompetence. The five dollars you can keep. I have lots of money, just like Pippi, only mine's real. I inherited some from my grandma when she died two years ago."

The boys were no less confused when she stopped talking than they had been when she began.

"So anyway, obviously you don't have to confront me anymore," she continued. "I kind of beat you to that."

Baron finally said something. "But why?"

It was a small question as far as words go, but it summarized every thought that was floating around in his head, and it nailed the big unknown as to why she had come to them in the first place.

"You mean, why did I come to you in the first place if everything I said was a lark? Okay. That's fair. Here's the deal:

I'm new in town. I have no friends. I'm bored out of my skull. All I do all day is sit around, read books, watch TV and listen to two middle-aged women whine about their pitiful lives. When I saw your little advertisement pinned to the bulletin board in the grocery store I thought, Hey, cool. Maybe I'll give these guys a try. I assumed right away you were guys, for some reason. That bothered me a bit. But I'm looking for something to do. I have space in my life and I want it filled. Detective work sounds interesting — in a nerdy kind of way. But I have no problem with that."

Baron stared at her in astonishment. "You mean you want to join our agency?"

"Basically, yes. Should I have just said that?"

"Are you serious?"

"I'm always serious. Well, okay, maybe not always always. But yes, I'm serious. I'm also smart, clever and tough. And, as you already know, I'm very sneaky."

"But you lied to us."

"So what? It's part of the business, isn't it? Besides, I had to see what you two were all about. And I must admit, you figured out my scam pretty quickly. Hats off to you for that." She motioned toward Myles, who accepted her comment with a brief blush of gratitude and then quickly checked himself and looked angry again.

"I don't know about this," said Baron. In his daydreams, he almost always worked alone. Myles was an irritating neighbor down the hall or a firearms specialist who was called in as required. There had never been room or reason for a female associate. On the other hand, he could not deny that he was enjoying the side of her that he was seeing now. Her spunk. The way she talked. Her shiny smile.

"First of all, which one of those twelve names is the one you go by?" Myles stepped back into the fray.

"Well, Sharla was a joke, right? I'm surprised you didn't say anything about the Sharla, Carla, Marla thing. But anyway. I was thinking last night that it might be cool to go by my last name. Wilson sounds tougher than Rebecca. Plus, it'll make people even more surprised when they see that I'm a girl."

Myles cleared his throat and rolled his eyes. "Okay, *Wilson*. Second of all, forget it. We're a two-man operation here, period. If we want someone to join us, we'll put the word out. Third of all, if we did put the word out, you would be the last person on earth we'd pick."

"How come?"

"Because. That's how come."

"That's not a reason."

"Sure it is."

"Is it because I'm better than you?"

"What are you better at than me?"

"Umm…everything? Thinking. Figuring out things. Karate."

Myles narrowed his eyes again. "We haven't proven that one yet."

"Oh, get off it. I'd turn that curly little head of yours

inside out with one hand tied behind my back. Now, cut the guff. You two talk it over and decide. Baron here doesn't seem to mind my idea."

Baron agreed that they should talk. He pulled Myles aside. "She's not all bad," he began, even though he wasn't completely sure. "Maybe she'll have some new ideas on how we can get more business."

Myles was having none of it. "Are you out of your mind? She'll tear us apart. Didn't you hear the way she was talking to me? 'I'll turn your curly little head inside out.' That's verbal abuse! She's uttering threats! I could have her charged for saying that."

"She was scared," said Baron. He knew how to handle Myles when he got excited.

"Scared?"

"Yes."

"Of what? Of me?"

"Yes."

"You think she's scared of me?"

"Of course I do. You're very intimidating when you get angry. You forget that about yourself sometimes."

"That's true."

"You have her saying things she doesn't mean."

"What about this, then? She's homeschooled."

"So?"

"So? She has no social skills. She can't interact with other people."

"Come on. That's not true."

"It is true. Look what she's said to us so far. She's lied. She's called me names."

"People at school call me names everyday."

"No, they don't."

"They do so. They call you names too."

"That's different."

"No, it's not."

"Yeah, it is. It's totally different. We go to school with those guys. We share a bond. We have nothing in common with her."

"I say we take her up on it." Baron wanted the discussion to end. He was suddenly excited about the prospect of adding a third member to the agency.

"You're crazy."

"We give her a three-month trial period, subject to review. If it's not a unanimous decision at the end, she goes."

Myles thought for a moment. It was true that business had been slow lately, and she *had* complimented him on how quickly he'd figured out her story about the blue whale. But could they really accept her as a new partner?

"Two months," he said.

"Deal." They shook hands and turned back to Wilson.

"You're in." Baron was unable to contain his smile. Wilson beamed back. Myles continued to frown.

"In two months we'll review our decision," Baron continued. "We'll see how well we're working as a group of three instead of two."

"Sounds fair," said Wilson. "Maybe we'll decide to get

rid of him." She pointed to Myles, whose jaw dropped like a brick off the back of a truck. "I'm joking. Come on. Don't be so serious all the time. Don't be so much like your dad."

Before Myles could respond, Baron stepped in with another question.

"What's this gonna do to the name of our agency now? It was the C&M Detective Agency before. Should we leave it or change it for two months and see how it goes?"

"We should leave it," said Myles.

"No, let's change it," said Wilson. "I have the perfect name. The Blue Whale Detective Agency. I love it."

Myles's eyebrows shot straight up his forehead.

Baron thought for a moment. "What's it mean?"

"It doesn't mean anything," said Wilson. "It's just a name, but I like it because it was a blue whale that brought us all together, right? So even if this doesn't work, we can call ourselves the Blue Whale Detective Agency for the next two months."

"It was an imaginary blue whale that brought us together," corrected Myles. "A whale that doesn't even exist."

"Whatever," said Wilson.

"I like it," said Baron, who was thoroughly enjoying the company of his new partner. "Let's change it."

He smiled again at Wilson, who smiled back.

Myles's face remained somber. He silently made it his mission to find out more about Wilson, because what she was telling them was still not making enough sense.

CHAPTER FOUR

Ironically, Rebecca felt worse, not better, as she rode home after her meeting with Baron and Myles.

True, she had gotten what she wanted: two new friends, plus something — detective work — to actually look forward to when she woke up in the morning. But she had lied about her sister, and that made her feel rotten all over again.

"Sorry, Pamela," she said out loud as she steered her bike down Main Street toward her aunt's house.

She did not expect to hear a reply, but she knew what Pamela would have said: "Just don't do it again. I may be dead, but I can still kick your butt if I want to. Remember, I already have my black belt."

A year ago, Rebecca's life had been a lot different. She'd been in grade six at Strathmillon Elementary School in Winnipeg. She'd played volleyball and basketball and had loads of friends.

Her mom and dad were going through the final stages

of their divorce, but even that wasn't so bad because finally, with the end in sight, they were actually starting to get along with each other.

Then her older sister, Pamela, had been killed in a car accident. Eighteen years old, on the brink of graduation and eager to get on with the rest of her life, her car was T-boned by a drunk driver who missed a stop sign.

The two girls had been very close, drawn together as allies as their parents' marriage noisily fell apart. They shared secrets. They talked about their dreams.

Pamela had wanted to be a writer, but she hadn't known how to tell their mom and dad. They were pushing her to train as something practical, like a nurse or, at the very least, a lab assistant.

"Nursing is something you'd be very good at," their mother had said. "That's why you should do it."

"Good at what, giving needles to people? I should feel happy about that?"

"Of course you should. You think just anybody can do that?"

"Who cares? I hate people who give me needles. I don't want people to hate me. If I wanted that I'd be a teacher."

Rebecca loved the stories Pamela wrote. Her favorite was about a blue whale who loved tourists. He loved them so much that every time he saw a boat full of whale-watchers he swam toward it. He was on television and in newspapers around the world. The media called him a modern-day Moby Dick because they thought he was dangerous.

Eventually the whale was killed. The hunters who did the job were hailed as heroes. No one understood that he was just trying to be friendly.

Rebecca cried when she read the story the first time. "He was so misunderstood," she sobbed. "No one listened to him."

"He couldn't talk." Pamela had been less enchanted with the story but believed it had potential. "It's supposed to be funny."

"I want you to rewrite it and put me in it so I can tell everyone what he's trying to do," said Rebecca.

"That's actually not a bad idea. Let me think about it."

A month later, Pamela was dead.

Rebecca turned up her aunt's driveway and parked her bike along the side of the house, where she'd been told to put it.

"Thank you for not hating me for talking about you the way I did."

She talked to Pamela all the time, usually in her head but, on occasion, out loud. It was one of the benefits of being schooled at home: She could say whatever she wanted without anyone hearing her.

The grief counselor her mother had arranged for her to see said it was perfectly fine for her to carry on this way. "It's called expanding your relationship with the deceased. Your sister may not be with you physically anymore, but she will always be your sister. Her spirit can stay with you forever. You can talk to her. Laugh with her. Cry with her."

Still, it was complicated.

Too complicated sometimes.

The questions she wanted to ask Pamela haunted Rebecca every day of her life: Why didn't you just stay home that night? We were having fun. Mom and Dad weren't fighting. And why couldn't you have waited for Kendra to pick you up, instead of getting impatient and leaving on your own? Why did you have to pick that exact time to go out?

She had other questions too. Why did the drunk have to go the way he did? He hadn't even known the neighborhood. He told the police that he was just driving around, looking for a store to buy cigarettes. Why didn't he see the stupid stop sign?

She went inside her aunt's house, removed her shoes and put them where they belonged on the shelf behind the back door. There was no one else home. Auntie Heather was at work. Her mom was out looking for a job.

She plugged in the kettle to make herself a cup of tea. There was a new note on the refrigerator: *Rebecca, please remember to keep your clothes away from Cassandra's in the closet. She does not want you to get them mixed up!*

This was not a cheery reminder. It was a warning.

Cassandra was Rebecca's cousin. She was away at university, taking extra spring and summer courses at McGill so she could begin work on her Masters degree sooner. Cassandra was twenty-three and very smart. Actually, she was very everything — beautiful, intelligent, gifted, snobbish, conceited and cold.

Pamela had hated her. She called her Cassandra the Great, and in one of her stories she made her a queen whose head was chopped off when the King grew tired of her whining.

Rebecca was staying in Cassandra's bedroom. Her aunt had told her many times where she could put things and where she could not.

"You can use the computer desk but this little filing cabinet over here remains closed at all times. Do you hear me? This little filing cabinet remains closed at all times." Auntie Heather could be reasonably nice sometimes. Mostly, though, she was a witch.

"You can put your clothes here and here, but not over there and not in there. This side of the closet is fine. That side is not. Do you understand, or do I have to say it again?"

She also had very high standards of cleanliness.

"I expect you to vacuum in here a minimum of once a week. The sheets come off the bed and go downstairs by the washing machine every Thursday before I leave for work. You can pick them up Thursday night and put them back on your bed. There will be no food in here at any time. Beverages are restricted to water and herbal tea. If there's milk or cream in it, you drink it downstairs at the kitchen table. Where do you drink it? Downstairs at the kitchen table."

Rebecca's mother, Joanne, promised they would move out as soon as they could, but finding a decent job was proving to be harder than she had thought it would be.

Rebecca poured herself a cup of tea, added cream and a lump of sugar, and took it upstairs to her cousin's bedroom. In honor of Pamela, she was intent on breaking as many rules as she could without getting caught.

She sat on Cassandra's bed and felt waves of anxiety wash over her like the waves on the beaches she and Pamela used to play on in Nova Scotia.

She sipped her tea.

"So what do you think of my new friends?"

The silence was deafening.

"I like them. I think Baron is nice. Myles may take a little getting used to, but that's okay."

She set her cup down on the duvet.

"I told them I was looking for a blue whale. They had no idea what I was talking about. I'm probably going to tell them at some point. I don't know. Maybe I won't. I know you used to say, 'Don't tell anyone what I'm writing until I say I'm done.' This time might be a bit different though. We'll see. At least I'm not the nutcase I was yesterday. Did you see me in that little office? God. I was crazy. Today I was much better. Way better."

The phone rang. It was probably her mom, checking up on her, or her aunt, telling her to preheat the oven for supper or wash a head of fresh lettuce for a salad or run the dishwasher.

Rebecca picked up her tea and went down the hall to answer the phone. She was in no mood to talk to anyone, but there would be too many questions if she ignored it.

Besides, maybe it was Baron or Myles calling to see if she got home okay.

It was a long shot that it was someone other than her mom or her aunt, but at least now it was a possibility.

CHAPTER FIVE

They reconvened in the office on Friday after school to discuss policies and procedures.

"Policy number one," said Myles, who had called the meeting to order and prepared its agenda. "All cases shall be treated with utmost confidentiality." He looked up from the notebook he was reading from. "That means no blabbing outside the office."

Baron and Wilson, sitting beside each other beneath the window, nodded their understanding.

"Number two. All cases shall be discussed and agreed upon by all members prior to commencement of investigation.

"Number three. At any time, a case may be dropped from the roster if members deem it to be unworthy, unmanageable, unsafe or damaging to our reputation in any way, shape or form."

Baron, who had been through this process many times before, nodded vacantly again. Wilson thought for a moment, and then she raised her hand to ask a question.

"Number four," proceeded Myles.

"Excuse me," said Wilson.

Myles briefly glanced up from his notebook before he returned to his notes and repeated himself. "Number four."

"Hey." Wilson dropped her hand. "Don't ignore me."

"He's not ignoring you," said Baron in a loud whisper. "One of the policies to come is that no one can ask questions while he's reading the policies. He likes to stay focussed."

"Number four," Myles went on. "While a peaceful and successful conclusion is the primary goal of every investigation, consideration will be given at all times to the safety and security of the agency's members. Termination of any case shall be administered if said safety and security is jeopardized.

"Number five. Moneys spent and/or collected during the investigation of any case shall be documented accurately and honestly.

"Number six. All investigative work shall be conducted with professionalism, including manner of speech, dress and the showing of proper respect to all related and, when required, unrelated authorities.

"Number seven. All confidential information gathered and recorded during the investigation of any case shall be kept in the possession of members of the agency only.

"Number eight. All physical altercations shall be documented and investigated internally and, when required, externally.

"Number nine. No eating in the office.

"Number ten. There shall be no interruptions during the reading, writing or revising of the policies and procedures. Time will be given later for discussion and/or possible amendments."

Myles looked up from his notebook after reading the tenth policy. "This concludes the reading of the policies. Any questions?"

Baron wearily shook his head again.

Wilson shot her hand in the air as if she was catching a line drive.

"Yes?" said Myles.

"Why is the no talking policy at the bottom of the list when it should be at the top, so anyone listening knows not to say anything?"

The two boys looked at each other.

"That's a good point," said Baron.

"Yes, it is," said Myles. "I'll make a note to move it." He hunched over his notebook and made a note to move policy number ten to the top of the list.

"Can I ask another?"

"Shoot," said Baron. He liked having Wilson in the office again. He had thought about her all day at school. In fact he had thought about her to the extent that Mr. Phelps, his Social Studies teacher, had scolded him for "wandering" again.

"What do you mean when you say, 'When required, physical altercations should be investigated externally'?"

"If it's bad, we call a doctor." Baron was used to translating Myles's work. "If it's nothing serious, we just report it to each other."

"Have you ever had to call a doctor before?"

The boys nodded in unison. "Quite a few times, actually," said Baron.

"For what?"

"For him, mostly." Baron motioned to Myles.

Wilson looked at Myles. "What's been done to you that's required medical attention?"

"Well." Myles took a moment to organize his thoughts. "I had my nose broken last year by Jason Armour after I proved he was cheating on his girlfriend. Evelyn Warburg pushed me down the stairs at school when I told her mother she was smoking. Mac Arnason's dog bit me on the leg after he intentionally let it off its leash. Willy Taylor stuck a stick in the spokes of my bicycle when I was riding past his house, and I nearly lost all my teeth. Those were the times I was rushed to the doctor's. There's a whole bunch of other times that I didn't go to the doctor right away, but I probably should have. Like when Teddy Derkatz hit me in the back of the head with a frozen apple or when Jenny Mapleton stabbed me with her pencil."

Wilson was stunned. "These people did these things to you just because you're a detective?"

"Not necessarily, no," said Myles.

"Sometimes they just do things because they don't like him," said Baron.

Wilson frowned. "You're kidding."

"Not everyone out there likes Myles," said Baron. "He has a tendency to rub people the wrong way."

"That I can believe," said Wilson. "But still."

"I am who I am," said Myles. "My dad tells me it's good practice."

"For what?" said Wilson.

Myles shrugged his shoulders. "I'm not sure. He just tells me it's good practice for anything."

After a short break, during which, in accordance with policy nine — no eating in the office — they stood outside and ate chocolate chip cookies, Myles went through the procedures for handling investigations, beginning with the referral process.

"Referrals come to us by fax, e-mail, phone or in person. Either way, we don't move on them until they've been confirmed as legitimate, which is to say, until we have the referee's signature confirming the referral. Following confirmation, we meet here in the office and discuss next steps and methods of operation, which can include, but are not limited to, stakeouts, tailing, going undercover, fact-checking, eavesdropping, researching, interviewing and basically doing whatever we can to resolve the situation. We file a written and/or verbal report with the client a minimum of once a week. When the case is complete or the client calls off the investigation, we close the file. Any questions?"

Once again, Wilson put her hand up.

"Yes?" said Myles.

"You actually tail people and listen in on their conversations?"

"If need be, yes."

"Isn't that against the law?"

"We are the law."

"No, you're not."

"We pretend to be. That's been good enough so far."

Wilson sat back in her chair and shook her head. "That probably explains why so many people have tried to hurt you."

Myles shrugged his shoulders. "If you're good, you don't get caught."

"Where does that put you?"

"Actually, I'm very good. I've never been caught spying on anyone. It's when I file the final report that people like Jason Armour get upset. I followed him all over the place. I watched him make out with this girl who was not his girlfriend. I even took a picture of them holding hands over by the lake. He never knew a thing. Not until I told his real girlfriend, Melissa Winchester, who had hired us in the first place, and she told him how she'd found out. Then he punched me in the face and broke my nose. Evelyn Warbourg had no idea how her mom found out she was smoking until her mom told her. Even then she didn't believe it until I confirmed it for her."

"You told her you spied on her?"

"It's a moment of pride when you tell someone you've

been following them for days without being detected. I felt good about that. Even after she pushed me down the stairs I felt good about that."

Wilson turned to Baron, a troubled look on her face. "How come nothing bad has ever happened to you?"

"He has epilepsy and two older brothers," said Myles. "Everybody either feels sorry for him, or they're scared they'll get beat up."

Baron nodded his agreement and added ruefully, "Not many people feel sorry for me though, unfortunately."

"The funny thing is," continued Myles, "that his oldest brother, Martin, wouldn't hurt a flea and his other brother, Jeremy, would rather beat Baron up than protect him."

Baron shrugged as he caught Wilson's eye. "I am who I am too, I guess."

He did not like to talk about his epilepsy. Experience had taught him that the majority of people did not know much about it. Worse than that, however, was that they all thought they did.

"You have epilepsy?" Wilson looked at him in a way he had not seen before.

"Uh-huh."

It was not a mean look or a frightened one, but it was more intense than usual. Baron briefly had the feeling that she was about to share something about her own life, but Myles, who rarely picked up on such subtleties, began talking again, this time about money, and the moment was lost.

"The final policy to review relates directly to fees for service," he said, sounding again like the CEO of a corporation with many more than three employees. "The way we set our rates is this: Whatever the client can pay, we charge. If the client cannot pay us in cash we will accept in-kind compensation such as baked goods, free movie rentals, pop and/or other forms of suitable reimbursement. Any questions?"

Wilson raised her hand.

"Yes?"

"What is an unsuitable form of reimbursement?"

Myles thought for a moment. "We've never run into one."

"We did last year, sort of," said Baron. "Remember when Cory Raulston told us she'd stop teasing you in Science if you found out who stole her calculator?"

Myles nodded. "That's probably about as far as we'll ever go in the direction of unsuitable compensation."

"What happened?" said Wilson.

"We got ripped off," said Baron.

"Did you find the calculator?"

"Oh yeah," said Myles. "Her so-called friend Wanda Whitaker took it."

"Did she stop teasing you?"

"For about a week. Then Wanda convinced her that she'd taken it by mistake, and we were all right back where we started."

Wilson had two more questions. Now that she was learning about the ins and outs and ups and downs of detective work, she wanted to know more about the history of the agency itself. Namely, how did it start and who thought of it?

"The C&M Detective Agency was officially formed two years ago." Myles began flipping through his notebook again. "I should have a copy of our mission statement here somewhere."

Wilson's eyes widened. "You have a mission statement?"

"Better believe it."

"Myles's parents are pretty intense people," said Baron. "They told him that if we were going to start an actual business — which we weren't, but they thought we should, even though we were only ten years old at the time — then we had to have a mission statement and a budget."

"A budget?" said Wilson.

"Here it is." Myles handed his notebook to Wilson. "I have copies of it at home. This is the original."

Wilson read the mission statement aloud. "'At the C&M Detective Agency, we are dedicated to providing our clients with the very best, top secret detective work such as spying, recovering stolen goods and solving mysteries. If you are not satisfied with the service we provide, your payment will be returned in full, with an apology.'" She handed the notebook back to Myles. "Very impressive."

"Gus and Moira helped us out," said Myles. "As for who started it, that was his doing." Myles pointed to Baron.

"It was just a game we liked to play," said Baron. "We called it Spying On People. We started out following my mom all the time. Then she got mad at us and told us to go spy on someone else, so we did. That's how it started."

"Then your sister hired us," said Myles.

"That's right. My sister, Kitty, hired us to spy on this guy she had a crush on. She wanted to know if he had a girlfriend."

"And?" said Wilson.

"We found out he didn't. Kitty moved in, had her claws into him in about a week and never paid us a cent."

"You're kidding."

"She's cheap." Baron shook his head. "She needs all the money she can get her hands on for makeup and lipstick. It's the only way she can ever get a date."

"You two sound really close."

"We're like this." Baron crossed two fingers together. "Just like you said you were with your sister, but she was just pretend."

Wilson looked stunned for a moment, as if she didn't know what Baron was talking about and couldn't believe what he had just said. Then she quickly recovered and gave him a brief smile. "Right. I forgot I said that."

An awkward moment followed. Then Myles got down to the next item on his agenda: introducing Wilson to the cases they were working on.

CHAPTER SIX

"First up is the Sandwich Artist."

Myles tucked away the red notebook he had been reading from and pulled a blue one out of his backpack. Across the front he had written in bold black letters: *CASES*. "Notepads out, everyone. This is a new one. There will be documenting to do."

Baron pulled a small coiled notepad from his jean jacket pocket and flipped it open. From his other pocket he pulled out a pen.

"You guys still haven't given me back that notepad I lent you," said Wilson, who sat with her hands folded on her lap.

"Don't worry about that," said Myles. "You can read mine. We'll be working on this together."

"Great, but I still want that notepad back."

"Absolutely." Myles began to read. "This case came to us from one Ronald Cooper, a grade eleven student at Emville High School. Mr. Cooper would like us to determine how much food his girlfriend, Julianna McCallister, also a grade eleven student at the same high school, is eating during her shifts at SuperSub. Apparently Ms. McCallister has been putting on an increasing amount of weight since she began working there three months ago. Mr. Cooper believes it's because of the sandwiches and cookies she's been eating, which she allegedly denies. We have an inside contact on this one — Baron's brother Jeremy works with Ms. McCallister. Jeremy has informed me, at the cost of two dollars, that Ms. McCallister's next shift is this Sunday from eleven AM to seven PM. At the cost of an additional two dollars, he informed me that her lunch break will commence at three o'clock sharp and will take place at the picnic table behind the store, where she prefers to sit so she can get some fresh air while she's eating. I took the liberty of scoping out the area. It should be an easy one for us. There are a few trees back there we can climb or hide behind. I'll bring Gus's high-range binoculars so we can gather all the information we need from a safe distance. I'd like to take Wilson along on this one — see how she does. In order to protect Jeremy's identity, I don't think it's a good idea for Baron to be involved." Myles stopped reading and looked up from his notepad. "Any questions?"

Baron, still writing in his notepad, shook his head.

Wilson, a look of renewed disbelief frozen on her face, lifted her right hand and said, "I have a question."

"Yes."

"Do you know what morals are?"

"What?"

"Morals, as in ethics?"

"Of course."

"Then why are we taking this case? This is disgusting. Spying on some poor innocent girl because her jerk of a boyfriend says she's getting too fat? Who's he — Bob the Body Builder?"

Myles's eyes met Wilson's red glare and held tight. "There's something you should know right off the bat, Wilson. This is a dirty business. Sometimes very dirty. You may as well get used to it, if you're going to be here long. We collect the garbage no one else wants to find."

"Well, you found the mother lode right here, didn't you?" Wilson shook her head. "And your dad is actually lending us his binoculars so we can do it? If my mom found out about this she'd hang me from one of those stupid trees you want me to climb."

"Judge not what people ask us to find, for what we find is judgment enough."

Wilson scrunched up her face. "Excuse me?"

"That's a little saying Gus passed on to us when we first started. Baron here will agree with me. The day we start passing judgment on our cases is the day we shut the agency down."

"So you never say no to anything?"

"Never."

"Not even if it's something really mean, like tracking a person's eating habits?"

"I didn't invent these people and their problems. I'm just trying to help a few of them out."

Wilson sat back in her chair and crossed her arms. "You can really pop a person's corn when you want to, you know that?"

Myles, who seemed to be enjoying the attention he was getting, nodded back. "I've heard words to that effect before."

"I bet you have."

"I take them as a compliment."

"They're not meant to be."

"As Chief Intake Officer, it's my job to introduce each case as it comes to us, break it down and devise a strategy. I take a lot of pride in that."

"Well, you're a real terrific little Intake Officer, let me tell you."

"Thank you."

"But I'm not feeling too good about this job right now, if that's what I have to do to be a detective."

"Not all cases are like this."

"This one is."

"I'll be there to help you through it."

"What a relief."

"If it gets too bad, you can always run away and join the circus."

Wilson's face fell into another frown. "What?"

"That's what Moira says whenever I get upset about something. 'Run away and join the circus if you think it's so bad.'"

"That's a very loving response."

"Moira's a very loving person, in her own way."

"This is your mother we're talking about, right?"

"Correct."

"And she has no problem with you calling her by her first name?"

"Never has before. Same with Gus."

"Do you have any brothers and sisters?"

"No. It's just me, Gus and Moira. That's the family."

"How sweet."

"We spend more time in their coffee shop than we do in our own home."

"Wow."

"We even set up cots there if Gus is too tired to drive home at the end of the day."

"That must be fun."

"I like it, except when Moira gets too loud. That can be a bit difficult to take."

"You should take her up on that circus idea sometime, you know."

"I have thought about it."

"I'd love to see your curly little head fired out of a cannon."

Myles smiled. It was the second time she had made reference to his 'curly little head,' and he had noticed both times. "I don't think they actually do that anymore, but—"

"Well, I'm sure there's a lion's mouth out there somewhere you could stick your head in or an elephant you could lie under."

"I like the trapeze acts, myself."

"That would work."

Baron, who had not spoken a word in the last ten minutes, took a deep breath to settle his nerves. Had he not been present to witness what he was currently seeing, he never would have believed it could happen, but he was present, and therefore he had no choice but to accept it as the truth: Myles was flirting with Wilson. Yes, he definitely was.

Until today, Baron could count on one hand the number of times Myles had engaged in a conversation with a girl, and those were all times when he absolutely had to, like when he was paired with Samantha Rollins in Social Studies to work on a project or when he was serving customers at the coffee shop. But as for chatting and making clever quips about his family? Forget it. One hand was five fingers too many to count the times that scenario had occurred. Yet here he was, right in front of his best buddy, chatting up Wilson as if the two of them were on a date. True, their conversation wasn't exactly lovey-dovey. But in Myles-speak, it was pretty close.

What was most galling to Baron was that for the first time in his life, he was actually thinking about a girl, and right before his eyes, his best friend was starting to take her away from him. Was that fair? Baron sure didn't think so. He'd been the one who had spoken kindly to her (not harshly, like she was some kind of criminal, the way Myles did) during their interview. He had not been the one to accuse her of lying about everything (the fact that she actually had been lying made no difference). Most of all, he'd been the first one to accept her request to join the agency. He'd been the one to say, "I say we take her up on it." Those had been his words, not Myles's.

Did any of that matter now? Apparently not. Apparently what mattered now was that they both liked the circus. "'I'd love to see your curly little head fired out of a cannon,'" he muttered to himself. Immediately he imagined Wilson and Myles arriving at the circus grounds together, hopping out of the backseat of that stupid military Jeep that Gus drove everywhere. "Good luck!" Wilson would say as Myles turned toward the Performers' Only entrance. "I'll be cheering for you!" Would they kiss before parting? Would she offer him a little break-a-leg peck before he got into costume? Baron could not even bear to consider it. Wilson would find her seat in the crowd and begin to worry. Baron could see the frown lines on her otherwise wonderfully smooth forehead, the worry in her clear, deep-blue eyes. Maybe she would play nervously with her long, thick glorious hair. He could see her clapping and hear her calling Myles's name. He watched her chew fiercely on her fingernails as Myles's curly little head (as she put it) was eased gently into the cannon. Would she say a quick prayer for his safe and gentle return to the ground? Probably.

Now he knew why his sister Kitty — sixteen and dating steadily for three years already — spent half her life crying on the telephone. Love was a vicious game.

"So where do you fit into all this?"

Baron heard the question, but he was too locked in despair to acknowledge it or to recognize that it was being directed at him.

"*Hello*?" Wilson turned toward him, putting her face mere inches from his ear. "Earth to Baron. Come in, Baron. I just asked you a question."

He brightened immediately when he saw she was talking to him. "Sorry?"

"He just had another seizure," said Myles. "It takes him a minute or two to get with it again."

"You did?" said Wilson.

"No, I didn't," Baron snapped, turning to Myles. "Since when did you know everything about epilepsy? I'm the one who has it, not you."

"Then you were daydreaming again. Take your pick." Myles looked back at his notes to see if there was anything to add to the Sandwich Artist case.

"I wasn't daydreaming."

"Well, you sure weren't listening to me," said Wilson. "My mouth is, like, three inches from your ear, and you still haven't answered me."

Baron felt terrible. He had ignored the first love of his life, and the lifeline that had been thrown to him —

by Myles of all people — was lying in tatters on the floor.

As he always did during times of extreme crisis, and as he never did when he was off in another world solving crimes as an ultra-cool private investigator, he turned blistering red and fell speechless.

"Hey, cool," said Wilson. "We made him blush. Wow. I thought I was the only person in the world who did that."

"No, he does it too," said Myles.

"And you don't?" asked Wilson.

Myles shrugged. "I guess I do. I don't know. Not as much as he does. He blushes all the time."

"Shut up, Myles." Baron's lips shook with rage. "I'm tired of you being Mr. Know-It-All all the time. The only reason Wilson's here is because of me, so I should be allowed to talk with her as much as you do. She's my girl, not yours!"

It took a few seconds for the full impact of Baron's words to sink in, but when they did, the reactions of the three members of the agency were profoundly different: Myles stared in bewildered silence at his friend. Wilson blushed and covered her face with her hands. With no deep hole in sight to dive into, Baron did the next best thing. He ran into his house.

"Uh-oh," said Wilson, breaking the long silence that followed.

"I had a feeling this would happen," said Myles.

He adjourned the meeting and arranged to meet Wilson at an appropriate time on Sunday to carry out their detective work.

CHAPTER SEVEN

After leaving the office, Baron ran straight upstairs to his room, shut the door and flung himself facedown on his bed. He was mortified by what he had just done. He was in shock. He felt like a fool. He wanted desperately to wake up and discover to his enormous relief that it was all a dream. But he didn't wake up and he knew he wasn't going to because he knew he'd been awake all along.

He felt sick to his stomach.

He rolled on to his back and covered his face with his hands. It was no better this way than the other way. The words, "She's my girl, not yours!" pierced his mind like a train whistle on a frozen prairie night.

He shook his head, and then he escaped into a daydream, where he knew everything would always work out.

The dame to his right was named Yolanda. She was thirty-something, had short hair that cost her a hundred and fifty bucks every two weeks to keep short, and a size-two waistline that cost way less than that every two weeks to feed. She wore brown lipstick, bright red shoes and black pants that looked as if they were put on with a paintbrush.

The chick to his left was Sky, a twenty-three-year-old Californian with a tan as golden sweet as honey and a smile that made you wish you could live forever. She owned one pair of sandals, two bathing suits and a sunhat that her grandfather had given to her before he ran off with his girlfriend to New Mexico.

Neither of them were supposed to be at Baron's apartment, but they had showed up at the door at the same time, so he calmly invited them in, recited a long list of vintage wines they could choose from, then poured them each a glass from the only bottle he had.

The scotch he saved for himself.

They sat, sipped and stared at each other.

Baron knew the peace would be short-lived.

"So, Baron, aren't you going to introduce me to your sister?" said Yolanda, taking her fingers for a short walk through her hair. "Or is this a pesky niece you haven't told me about?"

"I was just about to ask him the same thing," said Sky. "Except I thought you were an aunt of his. Or an old friend of his mother's."

Yolanda coolly put down her wineglass. "Isn't there a bonfire you could be sitting around right now, singing 'Kumbaya' with all your little friends?"

Baron began to wonder if he should do anything.

Without either of them noticing, he checked his watch. He had twenty minutes before his real date for the evening was due to arrive. Ginger was a leggy redhead who had danced in a chorus line on Broadway for four years before buying her own fishing boat.

Yes, he said to himself, it was definitely time to do something.

"Re-fill anyone?" He held up the wine bottle.

"I'd love one," said Yolanda.

"No, thank you," said Sky. "I've had enough already."

"Oh, come now," said Yolanda. "I'm just starting to feel comfortable."

"Anesthetized is more like it."

Baron poured more wine into Yolanda's glass.

"By the way," Sky added, "I happened to meet Baron around one of those bonfires you made fun of, so maybe you should start paying more attention to them."

"Oh, really?" said Yolanda.

"Yes, really."

"Well, we all make mistakes."

"We sure do."

Yolanda gave Sky an icy glare. "And I forgive him for his."

Sky returned it in kind. "I forgive him too."

They stared at each other as the temperature in the room dropped below freezing.

"Well, I forgave him first," said Yolanda.

"I forgave him most," said Sky.

Yolanda frowned. "That doesn't mean anything."

"Of course it does. I have the most to forgive him for."

"No, you don't."

"Yes, I do. Look at you."

"How dare you say that, you little tramp?"

"I'll say what I want, you skinny bag of bones."

Yolanda slammed her wineglass on the table. Baron winced but said nothing as she rose to her feet. Her eyes burned at Sky who was also suddenly on her feet.

"Baron, this will have to wait until tomorrow. I no longer have a desire to be with anyone tonight," said Yolanda, her nostrils flaring.

"Baron, call me when you have that chair she's been sitting in disinfected. We'll pick up where we left off the last time," said Sky.

The door slammed shut on their way out.

A few minutes later, after he had washed and put away the extra wineglasses, there was a knock on his door: Ginger had arrived.

There were few things in life he appreciated more than punctuality.

The knocking persisted. It grew louder. Someone was shouting at him.

Baron awoke with a start. It was his mother.

"Are you coming for pizza with us or not?"

He had to think fast. Friday night was Pizza Night in the Colfax household. In the old days, when his little sister,

Peep (short for Penelope), was still a baby, all seven members of the family would go to Zobrano's for a pair of large pizzas (one super deluxe with everything, one pepperoni) washed down with bottomless Cokes. Gradually over the ensuing years, the number of chairs needed around the table declined: Martin frequently worked Friday nights; Kitty and Jeremy preferred hanging out with their friends. Still, pizza night remained a favorite Colfax family tradition, even with fewer people.

But this night, Baron wanted nothing to do with it.

"No thanks," he said to his mom through the door.

"How come?"

"I'm not feeling well."

"Since when? You were fine this morning."

"I ate some weird fish at lunch today. I think it made me sick."

"From the cafeteria? Should I call the school Monday?"

"No, Myles brought it in his lunch. He made me try a bite."

"Should I call his mother?"

"No, she'd be insulted."

"Well, how sick are you?"

"Not very. I just don't feel like pizza."

Finally she agreed to leave, but only after he promised to call her on her cell phone should he get any worse.

Worse? He said to himself. There's a state that's actually worse than this?

He listened as they made their way out the door and down the front sidewalk toward Main Street.

When he could no longer hear their voices, he flung the covers off and set off to find a solution to his woes.

"Have you ever been humiliated?"

He stood in the doorway of his sister Kitty's bedroom. Kitty was sitting on the edge of her bed, wrapped in a thick white towel, drying her long brown hair. Steam from her recent shower was still wafting through the upstairs hallway from the nearby bathroom. Beside her on the bed were a curling iron and a hair straightener, both unplugged.

Kitty stared at herself in the mirror across from her bed as she finished drying her hair and set the blow dryer down.

She answered Baron without looking at him.

"I think you should go see Jeremy about that. Humiliation's more his department than mine." Jeremy and Kitty were twins, though not identical. Their mother often told the story of how they had gotten along just fine until Jeremy barfed on Kitty's head when they were three days old. From that point on, the two of them had been at war.

Baron stepped into her room. "Jeremy's not home. He's at work tonight."

"Phone him. It's quiet there. Only losers go to a sub shop on a Friday night."

"I'm not allowed to. He'll get in trouble."

"Then pass me the phone. I'll call him."

"C'mon, Kitty. I need your help."

Her eyes never left her image in the mirror. "Is it about that defective agency of yours?" she said. "Because if it is, I'm no more interested in it now than I've ever been."

"Detective," said Baron, pulling the rarely-used chair from beneath her rarely-used desk. "And, no, it doesn't. It has to do with a girl."

Kitty's eyes finally left the mirror. "Really?"

"Yes."

She shoved her hairdressing implements to the floor. "Come to Kitty," she said, patting the bed beside her. "Quick now. Come on."

With a mixture of reluctance and relief, Baron walked over and sat down.

"Now tell me everything. What you leave out, I'll make up and put in, so you might as well just get it all out."

Baron sighed and rolled his eyes. "I don't know if I'm ready for this."

"Okay, I'll start. You're in love with a girl who is really a guy."

Baron jumped off the bed. "What? Where did you get that from?"

Kitty smiled and patted the bed again. "That's what I mean when I say, 'What you leave out, I'll make up and put in.' Now sit down and try again. This is hard for you,

I know. Especially for you. The only role models you have in this house are Martin, who's more likely to fall in love with a tree squirrel than a woman, and Jeremy, who's more likely to just plain fall."

"What about Dad?"

Kitty's smile turned sour. "Baron, honey, as a general rule, kids should not take dating lessons from their parents. They're from a different world and a different time. They're old. They forget things. You listen to me now."

Baron reminded himself that seeking counsel from Kitty was in fact a good idea. She'd been dating for years. Plus, she wrote an advice column called "Ask Ivana" for her school newspaper. She used the name Ivana because she thought it was so exotic and sophisticated.

"Okay," said Baron, taking a deep breath. "It goes like this." He told her about meeting Wilson, accepting her into the agency, and the day's disaster in the office, leaving out no detail that he could think of for fear that Kitty would fill in the blanks with her own bizarre material.

When he finished, he gave a little shrug and sat silently on the bed. He felt even more crestfallen than he had before.

Kitty stared at him for a moment; then she asked him one quick question before getting down to business. "Did you say Myles took your girl away?"

Baron, the lump in his throat growing by the second, nodded his reply.

"Okay," said Kitty. "Myles who?"

"Come on, Kitty. You know who Myles is. Monahan. My friend. My so-called friend, anyway."

"You lost your first girlfriend to him?"

"Apparently."

"My God, Baron. That is not a good way to start."

"I didn't do it on purpose."

"That doesn't matter. Don't let this get out at school. You won't date again until you're a senior, and I mean citizen."

Baron rolled his eyes. "Can we get on with it, please?"

Kitty gave her little brother a reassuring smile and a pat on the leg. "Of course we can. The first thing you should know is that this kind of thing happens...well, not very often in exactly this way, and with a person like Myles I still can't believe it happened at all. But anyway, it did happen, and that's what we have to focus on. So your first step to a full recovery is — and this is the most important step of all — you have to dust off your little blue jeans, pick up your ball cap, get back on your horsey and ride. Okay?"

Baron frowned.

"Don't stop talking to her just because she dumped you, is what I'm saying. And definitely don't stop talking to girls altogether. This is just one person. She doesn't speak for everyone."

"She didn't dump me," said Baron.

"According to you she did."

"I never said the word 'dumped.'"

"Well, whatever. You said they made you feel invisible. I call that being dumped and believe me, I've done it to people before so I know what it must feel like."

Baron shook his head but continued to listen.

"Now the second thing. This is more encouraging. From what you've told me, you still have a lot of weapons you can use to win her back."

"Like what?"

"Like for instance, have you played the I-have-an-incurable-disease-that-may-take-my-life-someday card? Does she know anything at all about that?"

Baron stared at his sister. "But I don't have an incurable disease."

"Oh no?"

"It's not even a disease. It's a condition."

"Well, where's the magic little pill that makes it all go away then? And why haven't you taken it yet?"

"There is no pill like that."

"Then it's called incurable."

"No it's not."

"And who's that man you go see all the time at the hospital? The old guy with the beard."

"Dr. Turnbull?"

"What is he again?"

"He's my neurologist."

"Exactly. Does she know you have one of those?"

"No."

"Tell her."

"What for?"

"Baron, do you know how impressive that is, having your own...whatever? That is awesome."

"You just said I had an incurable disease. Now you're saying it's awesome?"

"Lookit. You have to change the way you think. Stop brooding over the fact that you have to take a few pills every day. Start turning it into a positive. My friend, Myra Thompson, fell down a cliff when she was twelve years old. Now she's in a wheelchair. She can't walk. Tragic, right? There is not a guy in our school who doesn't say hi to her! She gets a ride home with Derek Joiner every day! Myra has turned a negative into a positive. You can do the same."

Baron stared at the floor before responding. "That doesn't seem right somehow."

"Well, it's not quite on the same level as climbing a tree to spy on a girl eating a sandwich, but it's right up there. The point is, you have to work with what you've got. You're not tall. You're not strong. You're not athletic. You're not particularly handsome. You're not rich. You're not a brain. Your haircuts are not great. You don't know how to shop for clothes. But you do have epilepsy — use it."

"I came in here to talk to you about how to get over humiliating myself," Baron said, "and now you're telling me I should throw a cape over my shoulders and become Epilepsy Boy."

Kitty shook her head. "I'm not saying that at all, Baron. Wearing a cape to school would definitely not get you anywhere. My point is—you haven't lost anything yet. That's what I'm saying. You didn't humiliate yourself. What you have done, though, is let it be known that you have the hots for this Wilson girl. That's something you're going to have to deal with. Whether it involves Myles or not, I don't know."

"So what do I do about that?"

Kitty refocused her attention on the mirror. In particular, on her hair. "Let's talk about me for a minute. Straight hair or curly? I'm going to a party tonight at Rachel Miller's house."

Baron gave her hair a quick look. "Straight."

"How come?"

"I like it more."

"You think curly looks silly?"

"I didn't say that."

"Too schoolgirlish?"

"You are a schoolgirl."

"You know what I mean."

"I don't have a clue what you mean."

Kitty narrowed her eyes as she moved closer to a decision. "You said straight?"

"Uh-huh."

"Good choice." She stood up and plugged in the curling iron. Then she sat on the bed again.

"I said straight."

"I know."

"But you just plugged in the curling iron."

"I know. You got me thinking about straight hair and that convinced me to go curly."

Baron shook his head.

Kitty smiled. "Don't you see how a girl's mind operates, Baron? We're not like men. We're complex. If I had said to you, 'Go with straight hair,' then you would have picked up the straightener without ever thinking for another second about the curling iron. You would have just gone and done what I told you to do. But me — I focused on what you said and that made it clearer in my mind what I wanted. I saw straight hair, figured out that I didn't want straight hair, so now I'm going with the curling iron."

"That's fantastic."

"I think it is."

"How does it help me though?"

Kitty raised the curling iron to her hair. "You don't know this girl, Baron. You may think you do, but trust me — you don't. No man knows a woman that quickly. Now you might run around telling all your friends you know her. But the more you do that the dumber you look because that girl is just sitting there thinking to herself, What a moron. He thinks he knows who I am, but he hasn't even taken the time to figure me out."

Baron reflected on her words. "So I should just get to know her better, is that what you're saying?"

Kitty turned to see him better. "Don't sit down with your little notepad and fire off questions at her. Hang out with her.

Be relaxed. Find out what makes her laugh. What's her favorite kind of pizza? What's her favorite movie? Does she prefer curly hair or straight hair? Be nice to her."

"I am nice to her."

"No, you think you're being nice to her. Screaming at your best friend that she's your girl is not being nice to anybody."

"I saw her smile."

"She was flattered. But she also probably felt pretty weird and by now she probably wishes she'd never hooked up with you guys in the first place, which is how I'd be feeling if I was sitting in some wooden shack with this little curly-haired creature telling me I couldn't eat inside."

"Myles is not a creature." Baron was ready to leave now. He'd found the advice he was looking for. "But thanks anyway."

"Well, he's not human," said Kitty.

"Wilson seems to like him."

Kitty grimaced when she heard that. "That should tell you something about her, you know. Maybe this girl isn't worth fighting for."

"Oh, she is." Baron began to walk out of her room.

"You better make sure. Myles is your best friend. You don't want to lose him for nothing."

CHAPTER EIGHT

On Sunday, from up in the tree, Myles checked his watch and made a mental note that Wilson was now officially late for her first assignment.

Not an impressive beginning to her career as a private investigator.

For the record — and this information had all been recorded, checked and now rechecked — the time was 2:31 PM. The sky was slightly cloudy. The temperature was twenty-three degrees Celsius, with an expected high of twenty-four. There was a sixty percent chance of showers overnight.

The subject of their investigation, Julianna McCallister — short dark hair, dark-rimmed glasses, name tag on the left side of her uniform — was due to arrive at the afore-mentioned picnic table to commence her lunch break in approximately twenty-nine minutes, give or take a minute or two, depending on how punctual she was and whether she was making a customer a sandwich or not when her break time arrived, and if so, which kind of sandwich it was and how quickly she could make it.

Myles was decked out in camouflage attire: green military fatigues with a matching hat and black steel-toed boots. He carried Gus's high-powered binoculars, a notepad and pencil, a jack knife, a canteen filled with water and a glow-in-the-dark waterproof watch, which he'd received as a Christmas present from Gus and Moira.

He peered through the branches again to triple-check what he already well knew — that his sight line to the picnic table, an estimated seventy to seventy-five feet, was perfect. With Gus's binoculars he could, if he wanted to, count the freckles on Julianna's nose, if she had any.

Behind him, at last, Wilson arrived on her bicycle. In accordance with the preparation package he had sent her by e-mail at 0800 hours yesterday, she parked her bike behind a clump of bushes approximately ten meters behind The Tree, as Myles had taken to calling it. She then climbed roughly fifteen feet up The Tree in silence, and drew up on his left side, coming to a stop on a branch that was easily thick enough to hold them both.

"You're late." He raised the binoculars to his eyes once more.

"Not really," whispered Wilson. In her plain white T-shirt and light blue shorts, she looked more like a girl on her way to buy a slush at the convenience store than a detective on a surveillance mission. Myles silently took note of her apparel and filed it for discussion at their next meeting.

"We still have twenty minutes before anything's supposed to happen."

"Supposed to happen," hissed Myles. "Many an operation has gone up in smoke because what was supposed to happen didn't."

Wilson looked around at their surroundings. "Why are we whispering? There's no one within ten blocks of us."

Myles took his left hand off the binoculars and put his index finger in front of his mouth. "Shh. It's good practice. Not all jobs are like this one."

"It's a damn good thing they're not." Wilson was still not in favor of the assignment.

"Don't swear. It's bad for your character." Myles let the binoculars dangle from his neck while he unscrewed the top of his canteen and took a sip of water. "Did you get my note about refreshments?"

Wilson rolled her eyes. "Did I get your fifteen notes you mean, about everything from bringing my own water to the time of the debriefing meeting on Wednesday? Yes, I got them. I've never had more e-mails in a single two-day period in my life."

"It's good to be prepared. That's all I was trying to say."

"I get it. Shut up, already."

Myles went back to his binoculars and scanned the area around The Tree, which was in an undeveloped field on the northwest edge of town.

"Have you heard from Baron?" Wilson interrupted his visual review.

"I got his e-mail, if that's what you're asking."

Wilson nodded. "I never knew he had his own neurologist."

Myles lowered the binoculars. "For about six years now. He doesn't usually talk about seeing him though. I don't know why he would have brought it up all of a sudden."

"Because he can't be at the debriefing that was scheduled for Monday. That's why we changed it to Wednesday."

Myles nodded. He remembered all that. He just didn't know why Baron was talking about his appointment. Usually he just went, came back and never said a word about it.

"Are you surprised he didn't say anything about what happened at the last meeting?" Wilson stared straight ahead as she asked the question, as did Myles when he answered it.

"Not really."

"Has he ever been like that before?"

"Not that I've ever seen."

"Are you going to ask him about it?"

"Maybe at the debriefing. I'll put it on the agenda."

Wilson rolled her eyes. "Not all matters for discussion have to be put on the agenda, you know."

"No, but this one should be."

"Why?"

"Because it has a direct bearing on the agency."

"How?"

"Well, if he's right, how can we all work together?"

Wilson hesitated. "What did you just say?"

Myles kept his eyes on the back door of the sub shop. "I said if he's right, how can we all work together? How can we function as an agency when two-thirds of us are a couple and the other one is a third wheel?"

Wilson could feel her blood begin to rise. "What do you mean, 'If he's right'? He's not right. I have more feelings for this stupid tree than I do for you."

Myles shrugged his shoulders. "If you say so." He had a small, barely noticeable smile on his face.

Wilson noticed it. "I do say so. I emphatically say so. I'll climb to the top of this tree and scream it until my lungs fall out. He is not right about us, Myles."

"Why did he say it then?"

"I don't know. That's why I'd like to talk about it."

"Then I'll put it on the agenda."

"I don't want it on the agenda. I don't want it to be official business that may have a direct bearing on the agency. I want to talk about it like normal people."

"All right." Myles raised the binoculars again. The back door of the sub shop opened and Jeremy Colfax's short thick frame appeared. He looked vaguely out toward the trees, gave the thumbs-up sign; then he retreated and closed the door.

"That's our signal," Myles said excitedly. "She's coming out."

Wilson wasn't interested. "So you agree with me now? This is not official business?"

Myles double-checked his watch and recorded the time in his notepad. "I didn't say that."

"What did you mean when you said 'all right' then?"

"I meant, all right, I'll put the question of whether it has a direct bearing on the agency or not on the agenda. Depending on how the discussion goes, we'll either refer it to the next meeting or talk about it like normal people."

Wilson nearly fell out of the tree. "You can't do that, Myles." Her face was on fire.

"Quiet." He raised his hand in caution. "She's here."

CHAPTER NINE

Julianna McCallister sat at the picnic table and plunked down the oblong bag that contained her lunch. From it she pulled a foot-long sandwich. Then she reached into her purse and withdrew a bottle of orange juice, a book and a second, smaller bag and put them all on the table as well.

She popped the top off the juice, opened the book, pulled a giant cookie out of the smaller bag and began her lunch. By Myles's count, she ate the cookie (he identified it as white chocolate chip) in eight bites. She then turned her attention to the sandwich — grilled chicken, he surmised, with mozza cheese, bacon, tomatoes, lettuce and possibly pickles. Her bite sizes were average, as was her chew-count, to the best of his knowledge.

"Chew-count?" Wilson's job was to record the data as he relayed it to her.

"The number of chews per bite. The average is between twenty and twenty-two. I would say she's within that range. It's hard to tell for sure."

Wilson shook her head and wrote down "average" next to "chew-count." She had not recovered from the conversation she had just had with him, but she had successfully put it aside for the time being.

"She's finished the first half of her sandwich." Myles quickly checked his watch. "It took her four minutes from first bite to last. Wow. She really gets down to it."

"Shouldn't you go from the first bite to the last swallow, since the sandwich isn't actually done until it's in her stomach?"

Myles pondered that thought for a moment. "Technically, you're probably correct. But I think bite-to-bite will give us an accurate enough reading of the situation."

"I was joking."

"What's that?" Myles was back to peering intently through his binoculars, watching as Julianna pulled a second cookie from the smaller bag. "A second cookie has been extracted from the bag. Another white chocolate chip. She's still reading while she eats."

"Why isn't her jerk of a boyfriend showing an interest in the book she reads instead of how much food she's eating?"

Myles slightly adjusted the focus on the binoculars. "Wow. That's a Stephen Hawking book. She must be into science in a big way."

"Should I record that, Doctor?"

"The client didn't ask for that information. I'm just passing it along out of interest."

Wilson shook her head. "Out of curiosity, does the client know how to read?"

"I'm assuming so. He's in grade eleven."

"That doesn't mean anything."

"Then it's not our business. How's that?"

"Does he know his girlfriend reads science books during her lunch break on hot sunny afternoons when most other people her age are risking skin cancer at the beach or hanging out at shopping malls?"

"That question was not part of the referral package."

"What is the client doing right now, by the way? Is he working like she is or hanging out with his friends?"

"My responsibility is right here. What goes on elsewhere is none of my business. Unless someone makes it my business, of course. She's just finished the second cookie. Six bites. That's an acceleration rate of two bites per cookie."

Wilson dutifully recorded the information, and then she did a quick calculation of her own. "You know what? If she keeps that pace up, she'll be able to eat her sixth cookie without even putting it in her mouth."

Myles did not respond.

"She ate her first cookie in eight bites, her second one in six, her third will be in four, her fifth in two, and her sixth in none! She'll be able to eat an entire cookie without even eating it. That's amazing. Good work, Professor." Wilson reached out and gave Myles a hard pat on the back to congratulate him for his finding. Myles, who was not expecting to be touched, reacted with a quick flinch and dropped his canteen.

It did not make a loud noise, falling the fifteen feet from the tree to the ground in the still and vacant lot, but since there were virtually no other sounds or sights for it to compete with, the sound was noticeable.

At least it was to Julianna. She looked up from her book immediately and, upon seeing something on the ground that hadn't been there a few seconds earlier, she rose to investigate.

"Uh-oh." Myles tracked her movements through the binoculars.

"Uh-oh, what?" There was a new look of concern on Wilson's face.

"We've got trouble."

"She saw the canteen?"

"She saw something."

"Is she coming over here?"

"She'll be here in about thirty seconds." Myles lowered the binoculars and looked at Wilson. "Think fast."

"Huh?"

"That's not good enough."

"Why me?"

He raised the binoculars back to his eyes. "Twenty seconds."

"Why are you saying that to me?" Wilson's eyes were wide. Sweat was beading on her forehead.

"Fifteen," said Myles. "Get going, Wilson. Do something or we're done."

Wilson thought frantically. Then she jumped from the tree. Myles, who had not expected her to do anything like that, nearly fell out of his own perch in surprise.

She landed with a soft thud on the scuffed grass and dirt below. "Whoops," she said loudly. "Dropped my canteen. Hi there. I'm Rebecca."

Julianna stopped ten feet from Wilson and frowned. "Hi," she said, her voice light and friendly yet curious. "Were you just sitting up in that tree?" She looked up into the tall leafy tree. Myles closed his eyes and prayed she wouldn't see him.

"Uh-huh," said Wilson. "It's my Reading Tree. I love to come here and read on days like this."

"Really?"

"I used to have one in my backyard in Nova Scotia. I just moved here three months ago. I miss the ocean terribly."

"Where's your book?"

"My what?"

"Your book? You said this was your Reading Tree."

"Right. I didn't bring one today. I brought my little brother. He's up there playing Army Man."

"Army Man?" Julianna looked again up the tree.

"You can't see him unless you come over here. See? There he is. Hi, Russell."

Julianna followed Wilson to the tree and peered up through the leaves and branches until she saw Myles crouched on the branch, looking terrified.

"Hi, Russell," said Julianna, waving up the tree.

Myles cleared his throat. "Hi."

"He's very shy," said Wilson. "He doesn't have many friends because he's homeschooled. Plus, he's big for his age. He's nine, but he looks at least eleven or twelve. And he's really clumsy. He's always hurting people when he plays with them."

Julianna moved in a bit closer so she could get a better look. "Wow. You really are Army Man. Look at the stuff you have up there."

"Yup." Myles tried to sound as young as he could.

"Those are neat-o binoculars you have."

"They're Dad's," said Wilson. "He's a real military nut."

"Wow." Julianna continued to stare up the tree. "You know, I have a little brother who would like to play with those. I bet he would be your friend, Russell. He's only seven though."

"That's okay," said Wilson. "That's all right, isn't it, Russell? You could play with a seven-year-old."

Myles briefly looked down and nodded his head.

"Sure you could," said Wilson.

"Does he like Lego?" said Julianna.

"He loves it. Builds with it all the time. It's a little freaky, actually."

"My little brother is awesome with Lego."

Wilson shook her head. "Russell would play with Lego all day if he was allowed to. Lego and Army Man, those are his two favorite games. And the circus. He loves going to the circus."

Julianna lowered her voice to slightly more than a whisper. "It's too bad he doesn't have many friends. He seems like a nice little boy."

Wilson nodded. "He can be. He can really get on your nerves sometimes too, though. It's partly his personality that keeps kids away. And the fact that he's so clumsy."

The two girls slowly moved away from the tree. Myles began to breathe an enormous sigh of relief. Then he saw Julianna bend down to pick up the canteen. She looked at it for a moment before handing it to Wilson. "Who's Myles Monahan?"

Wilson, her eyes nearly popping out of her head, panicked and dropped the canteen again.

"You really are a fumble-fingers, aren't you?" said Julianna.

Wilson picked it up and saw the bold black lettering across the flat surface of the canteen: *Property of Myles Monahan, Emville, Alberta, 959-1134.*

"He must be the previous owner." Wilson sounded calm again as she spoke. "We got this at a garage sale."

"You bought a canteen at a garage sale? I hope whoever this belonged to took good care of it. I wouldn't want someone else's germs."

"Hey, that's a good point," said Wilson. "Russell, do you know anything about the person who owned this canteen before you and Mom picked it up?"

From the tree, Myles rolled his eyes. "No," he called out.

"Was it a grubby house or was it clean?"

Myles cleared his throat again. "Clean."

"I wonder if he's any relation to the Monahan who writes for the newspaper?" Julianna frowned as she spoke.

"I don't know," said Wilson. "We don't know many people here. Why, is there something wrong with this person?"

Julianna answered with a shrug. "He's just kind of weird. He's this old guy who used to be in the military. Every time my dad reads his column he gets all mad and swears a lot. Monahan runs a coffee shop here in town with his wife. My parents said if they ever see me in there they'll take away my library card."

Wilson turned to the tree again. "Russell, was the person who sold the canteen to you nice or not nice?"

"Nice," said Myles.

"Which one did you meet, the man or the woman?"

"Both."

"And they were both nice?"

"Very."

"It's probably a different family then," said Julianna.

"Sounds like it." Wilson nodded.

"Although I'm pretty sure he referred to a son named Myles in one of his columns. The only one I ever read." Julianna glanced at her watch. "Wow. That went fast. I gotta get back to work."

"I'm sorry we interrupted your meal," said Wilson.

"That's okay. I was just reading. I can do that anytime. Sometimes my boyfriend comes here to meet me, but not today, so —"

"Oh, you have a boyfriend?" Wilson could not resist the temptation to find out more about Ronald.

"Yes, for now. I don't know. Sometimes I like him, sometimes I think he's a jerk."

"What is he right now?"

Myles flinched as he heard Wilson ask the question.

"Right now, I would say he's a jerk. He's all over me about my weight. He thinks I'm getting fat."

"You? You're not fat. What's he talking about?"

"He thinks I eat too many cookies."

"What cookies? I don't see you eating any cookies."

"The ones from inside. They're delicious. I could eat ten a shift if I didn't have to pay for them."

"Well, so what? It's your body, not his. And you're not fat. I think you look great."

Julianna took the compliment with a mixture of surprise and delight. "Why, thank you."

"I mean, those uniforms aren't the greatest, but I think you look just fine. Hey, Russell, come down here and tell us if you think Julianna looks just fine the way she is or not."

Myles froze in the tree. Did she really think he'd hop down and answer such a ridiculous question?

"Don't do that to the poor kid," said Julianna, coming to his defense. "Ronald's not a jerk. He just has some real jerky ideas sometimes. Anyway, I have to go. It's been very interesting meeting you."

"Maybe we'll see you again sometime," said Wilson.

"I'll look for you on the next sunny day. Bye-bye, Army Man."

"Bye."

"I'll tell my little brother about you. Maybe you two can play together."

"Okay."

"Bye-bye, Rebecca."

"Good luck with your boyfriend."

Julianna scooped up her belongings from the picnic table and went in the back door of the SuperSub.

Wilson, exhaling a sigh of relief, turned to get her little brother Russell out of their Reading Tree.

CHAPTER TEN

Tension was high at the debriefing on Wednesday.

Myles accused Wilson of undermining the goals and objectives of the agency by communicating with the subject of their investigation, and of putting his life in danger by practicing slipshod methods of detective work, specifically in the area of surveillance.

Wilson countered by telling Myles that it was high time they started being a bit more selective about the types of cases they took on, regardless of Gus and his little sayings. She reminded him that it was her "slipshod methods" that had saved his hide from being tanned.

"I beg to differ." Myles shook his head. "And if he was here right now, Ronald would too."

"What's that supposed to mean?"

"He called me last night. Apparently, after she got off her shift on Sunday, Julianna phoned and told him all about this really sweet but very weird girl she met on her lunch break, and about how this girl had reminded her that her body was her own — not his — and she could treat it however she wanted. He was real happy to hear that."

Wilson looked pleased. "Good for her. I'm glad she told him that."

"Now he's worried she's gonna run off and get tattoos plastered all over herself, or body piercings."

Wilson shook her head. "You know what? Ronald's sick. He's a control freak. 'Eat this. Don't eat that. Do this. Don't do that.' She should break up with that creep now and get on with her life." She turned to Baron. "You should have seen how nice she was when she was talking to Russell."

"Russell?" Baron had never heard any mention of the name Russell in the office before. "Who's Russell?"

"That was Myles's name after I jumped out of the tree."

"You jumped out of the tree?"

"I had to. It was our only way out."

"Out of what?"

Myles interrupted before she revealed the whole embarrassing affair. "Forget about all that. You weren't there. It's too hard to explain." He turned back to Wilson. "What you think of Ronald's state of mind is none of our business. He wants his money back. That's what I'm concerned about."

"Give it to him." Wilson crossed her arms.

"But we provided him with all the information he asked for. Julianna was finished eating by the time everything happened."

"What happened?" Baron had a bewildered look on his face.

"Nothing." Myles kept his eyes on Wilson. "In theory, we don't owe him a cent. He asked us for a detailed account of what Julianna ate for lunch, and that's exactly what I gave him, complete with chew-counts and approximate bite sizes, if you recall."

"So what's the problem?"

"The problem is he said he's going to turn me into his own personal sandwich-maker for the rest of my life, if I don't give him a full refund."

"Well, maybe you should try that then. You seem to think he's such a swell guy. The two of you might really hit it off. And you'd get really good at making sandwiches."

Myles shook his head. "I never said I thought he was a swell guy. I just said how we feel about him doesn't matter."

"It should. We shouldn't work for creeps anymore," Wilson said.

"We just have to be better at what we do so something like this doesn't happen again."

"Something like what?" Baron was getting irritated.

"Never mind," said Myles.

"You shouldn't have dropped the canteen. That's what started it all," said Wilson.

"Myles dropped the canteen?" Baron's eyes grew wide.

"You shouldn't have bumped me," countered Myles.

"We shouldn't have been up in that tree in the first place," said Wilson.

"You shouldn't have been allowed to join our agency without proper training."

"Proper training?" Wilson nearly exploded. "For what? You sat on a branch and looked through your dad's binoculars. Who needs training for that?"

"You do, apparently."

"No, you do, apparently. You're the one who couldn't hold on to the canteen."

Baron did not know what to make of it all. Obviously things had not gone well on the job Sunday afternoon. It sounded like there was a fair bit of confusion and that perhaps, as a result of everything, Wilson and Myles had discovered this was not a partnership made in heaven after all.

However, all that being said — and granted, no one had actually said it yet — he was once again feeling left out of their conversation, just as he had the last time they were all together. Wilson and Myles were practically speaking a different language, full of secret references and "You did so!" and "No, you did!"

Every time he tried to infiltrate their discussion, they slammed the door on his nose like a chef keeping a dog out of the kitchen.

"So give him half his money and tell him the other half stays with us," said Wilson. "It's better than nothing. That way nobody loses."

"What if he doesn't accept it?"

"Then we go to Julianna and tell her everything.

I guarantee she'll never speak to him again."

"Why should Julianna find out what happened before I do?" said Baron.

"Because it concerns her, not you," said Myles. "But we're not going to do that, so don't worry about it."

"Why not?" said Wilson. "It's a perfectly good idea."

"Because I'd be dead meat. That's why not."

"Oh, you would not."

"Oh, I would so."

"Well, so what? I thought you liked that kind of stuff—being pushed down stairs and punched in the nose."

Myles gave her a puzzled look. "When did I say that?"

"You didn't seem to mind it when you were running down your list of injuries the other day."

"That was for successful jobs. This one's a mess."

Baron bit his lip. He was tempted to ask again what had gone wrong, but he let it go. Let them play their game, he thought. It was time to get on with better things. He quietly rubbed his hands together in anticipation.

Baron had set a task for himself this meeting. It wasn't an easy one, but he knew he could handle it. With a bit more input and encouragement from Kitty, he had decided to use this debriefing session as the time when he would secure a date, time and place for him and Wilson to get to know each other better. Was that more important than finding out why Myles was suddenly named Russell for half an hour Sunday afternoon? He sure thought so.

On the business side of things, he had to find out more about a new case he would soon be working on.

"May I interrupt?" He raised his hand as he spoke, in an effort to be both diplomatic and firm.

"Please do," said Myles, looking weary. "Just don't ask what happened anymore."

"We have a new case to prepare for this week and I don't know much about it. The other thing is"— he took a moment to collect his courage —"I would like to ask Wilson something."

Myles hesitated before replying. He exchanged a quick glance with Wilson, who was looking just as curious as he was. Then he opened his case notebook and flipped to the newest assignment.

"All right," Myles said. "The new case involves one Tucker P. Worthinghouse. His mother phoned yesterday. She wants us to provide him with one-on-one supervision this Thursday afternoon while she goes into the city. Apparently his regular nanny is unavailable. His father's out of town. She can't find anyone else. He's seven years old. He goes to a private school in Edmonton. Thursday is a day off."

"You're babysitting?" said Wilson.

Myles looked up from his book. "Not exactly."

"What do you call it then?"

"I call it providing security. Like a bodyguard.

If the president of the United States can have one, why can't the child of an over-protective mother?"

"I'm not sure that makes sense, but anyway, so... what? You're going to put on dark glasses and talk into your shirtsleeve for the afternoon?" She turned to Baron. "Do you have a black suit you can put on and a really big gun you can carry?"

Baron shook his head. "It's not like that. I'll just hang out with the kid, make sure nothing happens to him. You could call it babysitting or you could call it providing security. Gus says it's like being a secret service agent. That's why we do it."

Wilson turned back to Myles. "Will Baron be working by himself or will he need support?"

Myles hesitated. "I was thinking it would just be Baron."

"That's no fair. If I worked with you, why can't I work with him?"

Baron turned red with excitement. This could be the chance he was looking for, without even having to ask for it! "She has a point." He tried to sound cool. "If she wants to work with me, why shouldn't she?" He was almost trembling as he spoke.

Myles gave him a cold stare. "You really want to know?"

"Oh, shut up," Wilson said. "That last job was as much your fault as it was mine."

"Baron knows that's not true."

"He doesn't know anything. You keep refusing to tell him."

"I'm not refusing to tell him anything."

"You are so."

"No, I'm not."

"Yes, you are. You haven't told him a thing."

Myles took a deep breath to calm his nerves. "Let's just forget about it and move on, okay?"

"See?" said Wilson.

Myles returned to the topic at hand. "If this job goes well, it could become a regular contract for us. Mrs. Worthinghouse is offering to pay six dollars an hour for a four-hour shift, beginning at four o'clock, sharp." He gave Baron a hard stare to emphasize his next point. "If this works out, she'll become our biggest client ever."

Baron nodded. He understood the gravity of the situation.

"We'll do the best we can," said Wilson. She turned and smiled. "Right, partner?"

Baron could restrain himself no longer. "Right." He beamed.

Myles closed his notebook and shook his head. "I'll try to convince Ronald to take half of his payment. I'm not in favor of going to Julianna if he refuses. We'll have to talk about that before we do it."

"Fair enough," said Wilson.

Myles extended his hand for a handshake.

"What's this?" Wilson asked.

"It's the way we agree on things here. Shake on it and it's done."

They shook hands. Wilson smiled as she prepared to leave.

"We just have one more order of business to take care of." Myles picked up his copy of the agenda.

"We do?" She had temporarily forgotten about Baron's outburst at the end of their last meeting and her subsequent conversation with Myles in the tree.

"What is it?" said Baron.

"It's about our last meeting."

In a flash, Wilson remembered. "Oh God, Myles. Don't go there. Just drop it. Everything's fine now."

Myles carried on. "It relates to the matter of relationships amongst agency members and whether or not we have an issue on our hands."

Baron also remembered. "Do we have to do that?"

"If it's on the agenda we do."

"But it's okay now. I don't even know what I was talking about."

"It's all in the minutes. It'll take two seconds to go over them."

"I don't mean I don't remember. I was just joking, that's all. I was kidding around."

Myles stared at his friend. "You weren't joking, Baron. You flipped out."

"It was an attention-grab. I thought you guys were ignoring me."

"Exactly. So is that an issue or not?"

"It's not. It was me, not you. I've dealt with it. I've sorted it out. I'm fine now."

Myles remained skeptical. "How did you sort it out?"

"I've talked with someone about it."

"Who?"

Baron hesitated. "None of your business."

"Was it a family member?"

"I don't have to tell you everything."

"Was it Kitty?"

"It was someone who helped me."

"If it was someone in the profession of helping people with their problems, I'll let it go. If it was Kitty, I think we should pursue it further."

"Back off, Myles," said Wilson. "If he says he's fine, let's just believe him."

Myles turned his attention to Wilson. "Have you met his sister Kitty?"

"No."

"Then stay out of it. Kitty only knows about a tenth of what she talks about. And that's a high estimate. Very high. She probably told him stuff that's not even true."

"Don't talk about my sister like that," said Baron, who had never defended his sister before.

"It's true. You know that. Anybody who's ever talked to her knows that. You can figure it out in two seconds."

"She's my flesh and blood," said Baron.

"That's about all she is."

"I would really appreciate you not trash-talking her, especially in front of Wilson, who has never even met her."

"Lucky you." Myles gave Wilson a quick look.

"I mean it," said Baron.

"He means it," echoed Wilson.

Myles took a deep breath. He stared at the agenda for a moment; then he crumpled it up and stuffed it in his backpack. "All right. It's not an issue anymore. It's all taken care of."

"Thank you," said Wilson.

"I'll pass on to Kitty that you now recognize her as an authority in the field of human relationships," said Baron.

"Whatever."

"I bet she'll appreciate that."

"I bet she won't understand it." Myles rose from his chair and swung his pack over his shoulder. "Good luck on Thursday. We'll talk again this weekend."

Wilson and Baron sat in silence after he left.

"Think he's okay?" Wilson spoke first.

"Oh yeah. He'll be fine."

"Does he really not like your sister?"

Baron shrugged his shoulders. "I think he has a crush on her. He just doesn't know it yet."

They picked up their bags and left the office.

"I wish I had a sister." Wilson mounted her bicycle.

Baron was too excited about the prospect of working together to take in what she had just said. "So Thursday? Right here? About three-thirty?" He could not believe how easily everything had just come together. "We can walk to the Worthinghouse job together."

"Sure," said Wilson.

He didn't catch the sadness in her voice.

He said good night and ran into his house, smiling all the way.

Wilson wheeled her bike through the back gate and rode home.

CHAPTER ELEVEN

Thanks to the fact that the notepad Wilson had lent them had her address and phone number conveniently scrawled across the back page, Myles knew exactly how to get to her house.

It took him only eight minutes to run home, get his bicycle, ride to Wilson's house and hide behind her garage.

The time had come to find out who she really was and what she was up to.

Two minutes and forty-five, forty-six, forty-seven seconds later — just long enough for Myles to catch his breath — Wilson wheeled up the driveway, parked her bike where it belonged, removed her helmet and hung it on the handlebars.

As she did on occasion, especially when she believed she was alone, she was talking out loud to her sister.

"All right, so I did it again. I said I *wish* I had a sister. You know what I meant, right? It's nothing personal."

Myles frowned as he waited for the reply.

"It's just that when I hear Baron talking about his sister like that, I really miss you. We used to fight like he does with Kitty. We used to talk all the time."

The clear, blue, daytime sky was ceding to night, but it was still not quite dark enough to provide Myles with the cover he needed to safely find out who Wilson was talking to.

"But anyway," Wilson continued. "You can't bring back the past, right? How many times have I heard that in the last twelve months?"

Myles sensed that she was leaning against the garage. He heard her sigh deeply. She seemed troubled.

"So what do you think of this Kitty person? Sounds like someone you could sacrifice in one of your books pretty easily. I'm going out with Baron on a job tomorrow. God, I hope it works out better than that disaster in the tree. I really don't know about Myles. Sometimes I think he's a neat guy and other times I feel like squeezing his head until I hear it pop.

"I know it's better than hanging around here with Mom and Auntie Heather. But still. I can complain about people if I want to, can't I? Isn't that one of the benefits of sharing all this with you — I don't have to worry about you telling anyone? There have to be some perks to this relationship."

She heard a sound to her right, turned her head and saw Myles staring up at her from behind the garage.

Immediately he ducked out of her view, leaving her with the impression that she was seeing things.

"Myles?" She picked her helmet off the handlebars of her bike and moved toward the back of the garage, where she heard a scuffling sound, followed by the thud of a heavy object falling to the ground.

"Myles, are you back here?"

She peered around the corner.

At first she saw nothing but a stack of rotten boards from an old fence that her aunt had replaced last fall. An old, heavy, wooden gate was leaned up next to the boards. Then the gate moved. Or did it? It was much darker behind the garage. There were no lights back there, only dense shade from the high fence that separated the neighbor's house from her aunt's.

Wilson stared at the gate as if she expected a monster to suddenly spring out from beneath it. She was spooked. Talking to a dead person could do that sometimes.

She raised her helmet above her head like a machete. "Myles?"

She waited and then swung down on the gate with all her strength. *Wham! Whamwhamwham! Wham!*

She stood, breathing heavily, and dropped her helmet.

For a few minutes, the gate didn't move.

Suddenly it shifted slightly, and then it began to rise slowly off the ground. Wilson bent to retrieve her helmet. Her hands shook. Her eyes widened.

She watched as the gate rose slowly and then fell awkwardly to the ground as Myles, covered from head to bended knees in mud, shook it off his back.

Wilson stared at him in silence. Her breathing slowed and then steadied. Her eyes returned to their normal size. She finally got hold of the helmet and clutched it in her arms.

"Hi," said Myles, his voice shaky. He cleared his throat. "Whatcha doin'?"

She swung her helmet, catching him hard on the shoulder.

"Ow!"

She swung it again and missed him. He raised his hands to protect himself. She kept swinging until he collapsed and hid under the gate again, like a turtle in its shell.

"You little creep! Stand up so I can knock your stupid head off!" She banged on the gate.

"I'm not going to do that."

"Get out here so I can stuff your glasses down your throat!"

"Calm down, please. I can explain everything."

"I'll bury you right here! No one'll ever find you! You'll decompose and be eaten by worms!"

"Come on, Wilson, let me get up."

"Stay there and die!"

Exhausted, she stopped swinging.

Myles poked his head out from beneath the gate. He saw Wilson slowly retreat to the middle of the backyard, where she flopped on the grass and covered her face with her hands.

He shucked the gate off his back and rose to his feet. Then he saw how dirty he was.

"Can I have some soap?"

Wilson lowered her hands and looked at him. "What did you just say?"

"I asked you for some soap. I'm filthy."

She shook her head. "You are an amazing creature, Myles."

"Right now I'm just a dirty creature. I wanna get washed up."

"Help yourself. The bathroom's down the hall to the right. You have to go through the kitchen first. If you see my aunt, tell her you were lying in the mud behind her garage listening to me talk to my dead sister."

Myles proceeded to walk toward her house.

"Are you kidding me?" Wilson was stupefied.

Myles stopped walking, turned and looked at her.

"Are you actually going to do that?"

"I wanna wash my hands."

"Wipe them on your face."

"Then I'll have to wash my face."

Wilson closed her eyes and took in a long deep breath of the cool evening air. "Stay out of my house, Myles."

"I thought it was your aunt's house."

"Right now, as far as you're concerned, it is my house, and I want you to stay out of it. If you want to get washed, use the garden hose. It's right there beside my bike."

Myles turned on the hose and washed his hands and face. "Got a towel?"

"Use your shirt."

"It's dirty."

"Then use your pants. Use your underwear. Wipe your face on the grass like dogs do when they're itchy."

Myles flapped his hands in the air and wiped his face with the sleeve of his T-shirt.

"That feels better."

"Does it?"

"Well, my shoulder hurts where you hit it, but…"

"How about when I was bashing you under the gate?"

Myles shook his head. "I had pretty good coverage under there, actually. It's kind of flukey how that worked out. The gate just fell on top of me when I was scrambling to get out of sight."

"Lucky you."

"It *was* lucky me. You could have killed me. Those helmets are hard, you know."

"Gee, I'm sorry."

"I'm surprised the whole neighborhood didn't end up back here. You weren't exactly quiet, you know."

"That's very thoughtless and uncaring of me, acting up like that with no reason. Oh, wait. There was a reason."

"The only reason you saw me was because I got careless. I heard you talking to someone and I wanted to see who it was."

"I don't mean that reason, Bozo. I mean you followed me here and spied on me. That's why I snapped my cap."

"You never would have known, if I hadn't gotten careless. That's all I'm saying."

Wilson stared at him for a moment. "So, are you here on your own, or are you acting on behalf of the agency?"

"That's actually confidential information."

"Oh, is it?"

"Yes, it is."

"Well, can you tell me anyway? Or do I have to get up and pound you again?"

"I'm really not at liberty to say. That's what I'm telling you."

"Myles, you were spying on me. You were trespassing on my aunt's property. That's illegal. I could phone the police right now, and they would be much more interested in what I had to say about you than anything you had to say about me."

"So?"

"So tell me what you're doing here."

Myles hesitated. "Why don't you tell me who you were talking to first?"

"You haven't figured that out yet?"

He pretended he hadn't heard what she had said about her sister. "You mean between crawling around in the dirt and being battered by a helmet, have I had a chance to reflect on any of the information I gathered? No, I haven't."

"What do you mean by 'any information you gathered'? How long have you been following me?"

"Just tonight."

"Are you sure?"

"Of course."

"What about Baron?"

"What about Baron?"

"Is he in on this too?"

"I don't know what you're talking about."

"Does he know you're here? Is he at home awaiting a report? I thought you two only conducted investigations after they were agreed upon by all members of the agency. Isn't that one of your rules?"

"It's called a policy, actually."

"Whatever. It's one of them, isn't it? But because I'm the subject of the investigation, I don't count, right?"

"No. That's not right."

"So that means Baron must know about it."

"No, it doesn't." Myles protested. "I'm here on my own. I didn't tell anybody I was coming."

"So you violated one of your own policies to follow me?"

"I guess I did, yes."

"And to find out what? Whether I have a sister or not? Whether I live with my aunt or not? Whether this bike is really mine or not?" Wilson's voice rose with every question.

"I came here to find out more about you. I was curious."

"That doesn't sound like you, Myles."

"What doesn't?"

"The part about you breaking your own policies."

"I forgot about them."

"See, that doesn't sound like you either. That sounds more like you're trying to cover for your buddy who's really just as guilty as you are of invading my privacy and making me feel like an absolute fool."

"You're wrong, Wilson."

"Am I?"

"Yes, you are."

"Well, we'll see about that. In the meantime, why don't you get out of here before I seriously hurt you, because that's really what I feel like doing right now."

"It's not anything like you think it is."

"Good-bye, Myles."

"Baron had nothing to do with this. This is not official agency business. I'm here on my own. I wanted to find out more about you."

"Like what?"

"Well, like first you said you had a sister; then you said you didn't have a sister. And when you did have a sister, she wanted us to find this blue whale. Then you said you went to school; then you didn't go to school."

Wilson narrowed her eyes in anger. "I told you the first time we met there were parts of my life story that I was not comfortable sharing. You could have respected that. Instead, you slithered around in the dirt and listened to me talk to myself."

Myles shook his head. "You weren't talking to yourself. There was definitely another person. That's why I came out from behind the garage."

"Oh, really?"

"That's what it sounded like to me."

"Well, where is she then?" asked Wilson.

"She's not here," said Myles.

"But if you heard me talking to her she must be nearby."

Myles hesitated. "Not necessarily."

"What's that supposed to mean? If you're so convinced that I was talking to another person, where'd she go? Where is she? I don't see her anywhere."

Myles gulped before saying anything. "You just said she was dead."

Wilson stopped talking.

"Is that the sister you were talking about?"

Wilson stared at the grass in front of her. "Yes, it is."

"Was she older or younger than you?"

"She was older."

"Did she really lose a blue whale?"

"She wrote a story about one once. It died. I was just trying to bring it back to life." She shrugged. "You weren't supposed to understand. I was just acting weird."

"Do you have another sister?" Myles asked.

"No, just the one. I talk to her like she's still alive, though. It's weird. That's why I lied to you about her."

"It's not right to lie to someone, you know," said Myles.

Wilson smiled. "Aww, that's so sweet. Did you learn that in Sunday school? I love it when adults say patronizing stuff like that to little kids. But you know what? It's not true. I told you that me and my sister do everything together. Did you accept that as the truth? No. You thought something fishy was going on. I also said I didn't want to talk about it. That was the truth. Did that get me anywhere? Not really. So you go back to your Sunday school teacher and tell her that sometimes telling the truth sucks because people either don't believe it, or they don't understand it, which is almost the same thing."

"I didn't hear that from my Sunday school teacher."

"Whoever."

"I don't even go to Sunday school."

"Good for you. Maybe you should start. You might learn something useful."

"Maybe I will."

Wilson took a deep breath in an attempt to steady her nerves. "You really can go now, you know, Myles. You found everything you were looking for. You can chalk this up as another successful mission."

"It was never about that."

"Say hi to Baron for me when you talk to him tonight."

"I'm not calling Baron."

"Whatever. E-mail him then. Send him a fax. Stick a note on his door."

"I'm not saying anything about this to Baron."

Wilson locked her eyes on his. "Is that the truth?"

Myles pulled his bike from behind the garage and rode home. Wilson sat in the grass until it became too cool to stay out any longer. Then she went inside, made herself a cup of tea and took it up to bed.

CHAPTER TWELVE

On Thursday afternoon at three thirty, Baron and Wilson met at the office.

Baron had barely slept the night before. There had been too much on his mind for him to sleep. Too many things to think about; too many things to do after he was done thinking.

"What's a good way to start a conversation with someone?" he'd asked Kitty earlier in the evening. She was in her bedroom, painting her fingernails.

"Depends. What do you want to talk about? Is it someone you *want* to talk to or *have* to talk to? Is it someone you'd like to kiss — or kiss off? Is it someone you'd like to talk to for a long time, like ten minutes, or is it a hi/bye thing?"

Baron rolled his eyes. "It's that girl I was telling you about the other day."

Kitty frowned as she continued to paint her nails. "What girl you were telling me about the other day?"

"The only girl I have ever told you about, on the only day I have ever come in here and told you about girls."

"Oh, her. Okay. What are you wearing?"

"What am I what?"

"Are you going casual? Semi-formal? Formal? Do you plan on doing any shopping first? Are you getting your hair done?"

"I'm walking to someone's house with her."

"In what?"

"I don't know. Shoes. Shorts. A T-shirt."

"Shoes, shorts and a T-shirt? The message you'll be sending her is, 'You are nothing special to me, see? I did not get spiffed up for you at all.'"

"We're doing a job together. I can't wear anything fancy. She'll think I'm nuts."

"Have you bought anything for her?"

"Have I what?"

"Have you bought her a gift of some kind?"

"Like what?"

"Oh, I don't know. At your age, maybe a bottle of nail polish, a hair clip, some fancy beads to wear around her neck."

"She doesn't wear beads or hair clips. She doesn't paint her nails either."

"Oh, really?"

"Yeah, really."

"You've seen her how many times?"

"Five or six."

"And you have her all figured out? Everything she wears and doesn't wear? Everything she eats and doesn't eat? Didn't we have this conversation before? You could always buy a box of Popsicles and stick it in the freezer, you know. When she comes over to the house, you can offer her one. Or does the fact that you've never actually seen her eat a Popsicle mean that she doesn't eat Popsicles either?"

Baron started to think. Perhaps this was a bigger deal than he had first imagined.

"Put some thought into this before it's too late, Baron. She probably is."

Inspired but confused, he'd tossed and turned in bed until the morning sun shone through his window.

At breakfast he asked his mom if she could buy him a box of Popsicles, changed his mind to Fudgesicles and then went back to Popsicles again.

He shampooed his hair, used some conditioner and put on extra gel. He tried on several combinations of shirts, T-shirts, pants and shorts before hitting on one that he thought worked: his khaki walking shorts, a light blue, short-sleeve, button-up shirt and his best running shoes, which he scrubbed clean with soapy water.

He also had an idea of his own. He consulted Kitty again.

"What about a book as a gift?"

Kitty frowned and shook her head.

"What's wrong with that? I thought it was perfect."

"The problem with giving someone a book is that they have to read it."

"That's kind of the point."

"What if she doesn't like reading? You've just given her a very unpleasant chore to do. It's like giving her homework or a pile of dirty laundry."

"What if she does like reading?"

"Buy her a kitten. They can sit in a rocking chair and grow old together."

"No, thank you." Wilson smiled politely as Baron offered her a choice of three different colors of Popsicles.

"Really?"

"I'm not hungry."

He took the Popsicles back into the house and rejoined her outside, but not before checking his look in the mirror for the tenth time. He felt good in his outfit. His hair was behaving itself. He'd chosen the right pair of shoes.

Back outside, he noticed that Wilson was wearing the same shorts and T-shirt she had worn the first time they'd met. What's that about? he wondered. Does that mean I'm nothing to her? Does she know something about fashion and sending messages that Kitty doesn't know? If she does, what is it? Should I ask her about it?

"So…" He smiled and decided to keep his thoughts to himself as they strolled down the sidewalk.

"So what?"

Wilson was clearly in a different mood than he was. Her face was sullen. Or angry. Baron couldn't tell for sure. Her arms were crossed in front of her chest. There were no signs of any playfulness or excitement about working together.

"Are you all ready to meet the demands of body-guarding a seven-year-old?"

"Whatever."

"Have you ever babysat before?"

"Of course."

"You probably have more experience than me then."

"I'm not worried about this job, if that's what you're getting at."

In addition to helping him get his head straight on what to wear and what kind of a gift to buy, Kitty had also given him four pointers on how to start and, more importantly, maintain a healthy and vibrant conversation with someone you care about:

1. Ask, don't tell;

2. Listen, don't talk;

3. Compliment, don't criticize;

4. Avoid conflict at all costs.

It was this final one that he suddenly found himself on the brink of violating.

"No no. I'm not concerned. Not at all. Look at me.

I don't have any concerns. I just meant, you've probably done things like this before, that's all."

"Things like what? Looking after a kid? Of course I've done it before. What twelve-year-old girl hasn't?"

"I know. That's what I'm saying. That's what I meant."

"What?" Wilson screwed her face up in confusion.

Baron stammered on. "That's...that's what I meant to say. What twelve-year-old girl hasn't?"

"I just said that to you."

"I know. It's a good point."

Wilson shook her head. "So why are you saying it to me?"

"What?"

"Why are you saying it to me if I already know it? I was the one who said it to you. I just said I've looked after little kids before. Now you're saying it back to me as if I didn't know that."

"I know you know. I'm just, that's what I'm saying. You know it already. That's my point."

Wilson stared at Baron for a moment and then rolled her eyes.

Baron, his face burning, quietly gasped for fresh air. Have I done something wrong already? Is she offended that I offered her a Popsicle? Have I thrown her off somehow? Instinctively, his mind wandered off to a safer, happier place.

He was alone in his office when his receptionist, Wanda, burst through his door.

"I wanna talk to you, buster!" she spat. Her makeup quivered like the side of a snow-covered mountain before an avalanche.

"I want to talk to you too," he responded coolly. "Come in and sit down."

Wanda, still fuming but now curious, took a seat.

"I know you're upset with me, Wanda, and I know why. I said you could take last weekend off, then I called you back in when that damn Mackenzie case broke. I was so busy getting that guy behind bars, I didn't have a chance to say thank you. That's why I bought you this instead."

He reached into his pocket and pulled out a gift card for an all-expenses-paid weekend for two at the fabulous Foremont Lodge on Crystal Lake in the Rocky Mountains. "You know I'm lousy with words. Here, take this. Call up Barry or Larry or whatever his name is and have yourselves a good time. It's for this weekend. Spend tomorrow packing if you want. I won't need you again until next week."

Wanda took the pass with one hand and wiped the tears from her eyes with the other. Baron hoped the pass didn't have his name on it anywhere. It was a gift from Martha Mackenzie, the wife of Big Ben Mackenzie, the thug Baron had just had thrown in jail for parole violation.

"It's Terry," she said, sniffing.

"Really? Who's Barry or Larry then?"

"Barry's my husband. I left him three years ago." She rose from her chair. "Thank you for this. All I wanted was a little recognition."

"I know the feeling," said Baron.

Boy, was that ever true, he thought as the daydream faded and he returned to his mission with Wilson. I could use a little recognition myself right now.

Silently he shook his head as he considered his current predicament; maybe he was the one who was off. He wasn't familiar with all this stuff about dressing for certain occasions and sending correct messages. In his daydreams of being a detective, he was who he was, period. He wore what he felt like wearing. He talked how he felt like talking. If whoever he was with didn't like it, then whoever he was with could leave.

Was this an approach he wanted to take with Wilson though?

"Did you see Myles at school today?" She interrupted his thoughts.

Relieved that she still wanted to talk to him and anxious to begin a new topic, even if it meant talking about the one person in the world he really did not feel like talking about, he lied and said, "Yes, I did. We had lunch together."

"Did he tell you about last night?" Wilson was staring straight ahead as she spoke. Her arms were still crossed.

"Last night?" Truthfully, Baron had not seen Myles at school all day, an unusual occurrence, but not unheard of. "A little bit, yes."

"I knew he would." Wilson shook her head. "What did he tell you?"

Baron reviewed the events of the previous evening: They'd all met in the office. Myles had left in a huff. Wilson had left on her bicycle. He'd talked to Kitty.

Something else must have gone on that he was unaware of. Wilson and Myles must have talked. Why else would she be asking about it? "He said that after talking with you, he...uh...he was ready to waive the probation period and make you an official member of our agency."

Wilson stopped walking.

Baron, who had not had any clue what he was going to say until the words were out of his mouth, stopped as well and tried to smile. "He said he wanted you around for a long, long time. And I agreed with him. Congratulations." He held out his hand for a handshake.

Wilson, stunned, ignored his hand. "That's all he said?"

"Well, that was the main point. That was the message he wanted to get across, I assume."

"Did he say why?"

"Uh...yes. He did."

"Why?"

"Why did he say why, or why does he want you to stay?" Baron tried to buy some time. He was not a natural liar, and Wilson's reaction was making him feel that being accepted into the agency as a full-time member was a much bigger deal for her than he had ever imagined.

"Why does he want me to stay?"

"Because...because...everything. You're good at everything. You can do everything. There's no reason for you not to stay. He said that and I agreed with him. Right away. In fact, I was agreeing with him before he'd even said anything, if that's possible. I thought of it first, is what I'm saying."

Wilson walked on, staring at the sidewalk.

Baron carried on beside her. "I was surprised when he said it because he had been so resistant to you joining in the first place, and then that first mission the two of you went on didn't seem to go so well, although no one ever told me much about it. But he's a funny guy, you know. As soon as you start thinking one way about him, he does something that gets you thinking the exact opposite."

Wilson showed no sign of wanting to say anything.

"I probably know him better than anyone else, you know," Baron continued. "It's because I'm so patient. My mom always says that about me. To her friends and the people in her writing group. I don't know. Patience is good, I guess. I'd rather be patient than impatient. I think it's better. I get impatient with my little sister sometimes, but not very often. My dad's patient. I probably get it from him."

He checked himself. Babbling had not been listed on Kitty's tip sheet. Besides, up until the end part, he hadn't even been babbling about himself. He'd been going on and on about Myles. What kind of a way was that to win a girl over to your side — talking up the competition?

He could just imagine what Kitty would say if she heard him.

"Well," Wilson cut in, "with what happened between us last night, I'm very surprised to hear that. Maybe I shouldn't be.

Baron quickly forgot about Kitty. "Something happened between you two last night?"

Wilson frowned. "Are you sure he didn't tell you anything?"

"I'm positive."

"Nothing at all?"

"Nothing."

She shook her head. "That's amazing."

"Why, did something happen?"

"Yes."

"After the meeting we had?"

"Yes."

"What, did you two get together after you left the office?"

"You could put it that way, yes."

"What did you do?"

"I'd rather not talk about it, if you don't mind. It's pretty personal."

Baron, his mind starting to swirl with thoughts and images, felt his face turning red. "You have to. You have to talk about it."

"No, I don't. Myles didn't. Why should I?"

"But if it's personal I have to know."

"It's personal to me, not you." Wilson shook her head. "I can't believe he didn't brag to you at least."

"Brag to me about what?"

"About his big successful mission."

Baron's eyes grew wide. "His what?"

"Never mind."

Baron could barely speak. He licked his lips so the words wouldn't stall halfway out of his mouth. "Let me get this straight. You two got together after leaving me behind last night?"

"I'm pretty sure I've said that already, but yes, we did."

"Where?"

"My aunt's house."

"Was anyone else there?"

"No, we were all alone in the backyard. Just me, him, a whole bunch of mud and a bicycle helmet. And it was all his idea. He followed me."

Baron tried to sort out the picture that came into his mind but couldn't. This was a story straight out of Kitty's demented world of high school relationships.

"Did it get…physical?"

"Very."

He nearly fell over.

"And apparently, it's not over yet. According to him, anyway." Wilson shook her head as she spoke. "Where is this house we're going to, by the way? I need something to get my mind off everything. It's been a long twenty-four hours, if you know what I mean."

Baron felt sick, but there was no way he was going to show Wilson how distressed he was. Never had he been so humiliated, so violated, so...he didn't even really know what those words meant, but the feeling in the pit of his stomach told him that something terrible had just happened.

"It's right over there," he heard himself say.

"Let's go, then." Wilson took the lead.

Somehow he followed, but as he did he vowed that as soon as this job was over, he would never again do detective work for the Blue Whale Detective Agency.

CHAPTER THIRTEEN

The Worthinghouse home was two stories of solid brick in the high-end part of Emville. It had a three-car garage and a circular driveway. There was a statue of a lion sitting on a pedestal in the front right corner of the lawn. The grass was exceptionally green and well groomed.

"Nice place," said Wilson as they approached the front door.

Baron did not respond. He could not have cared less what kind of a place the Worthinghouse home was.

Wilson rang the doorbell.

The front door opened. A tall, thin, frowning woman in a tan pantsuit let them inside. She introduced herself as Fiona Worthinghouse, Tucker's mother, and told them she was in a hurry. "I have no time for chitchat. Do a good job and I'll give you a bonus. If my son gets hurt or is traumatized in any way, we'll sue your parents. I'm sorry. That's just the way it is. It's the only way we can protect ourselves, short of hiring someone to watch you. But that's ridiculous."

Baron turned his head away and rolled his eyes. Of all the days to run into someone like this...

Mrs. Worthinghouse told them she would be out until eight o'clock. She gave them her cell phone number, plus a number where Tucker's father could be reached. "Try mine first. If I don't pick up, try me again. If I don't pick up the second time, call Mr. Worthinghouse. But don't expect much help from him. He's a busy man, and he gets very impatient." She picked up her purse from a bench in the foyer and opened the door. "Any questions? You get one each. I'm in a hurry."

"Where's your son?" Wilson asked first.

"He's hiding. His favorite game is hide-and-seek. I told him he could play it with you."

"Where does he like to hide?"

"Anywhere. The dryer. On top of the fridge. The laundry basket in the basement." Mrs. Worthinghouse slipped her feet into a pair of beige pumps. She pressed a button on her key fob and one of the garage doors began to open. She opened the front door and stepped outside.

"What about my question?" Baron's mind was gradually coming around to the job at hand, and he wanted to know if there were any rules they should be aware of, favorite playgrounds they should go to, snacks that Tucker preferred, medication that he had to take or allergies to be concerned about.

"Your colleague asked it for you. Remember: Keep your eyes on him at all times. If anything happens..."

"You told us that already," said Wilson.

"It's worth repeating, don't you think?" Mrs. Worthinghouse gave Wilson a menacing look. "I'll see you at eight o'clock."

A moment later, she backed a glistening black convertible down the driveway, turned up the street without waving and quickly disappeared.

"Wow." Wilson had a scowl on her face. "With parents like her, who needs kidnappers?"

Baron turned his attention back to the house and began to untie his shoes.

"You're taking your shoes off?" Wilson stepped past him with her running shoes still on her feet and walked across the carpeted living room floor. "I feel like putting gloves on my hands. What if she's contagious?"

With one shoe off and one shoe on, Baron stopped to think.

"I'm going downstairs to find whatshisname. I hope she didn't throw him in the washing machine." He heard Wilson open a door and go down to the basement.

He shook his head in frustration.

Briefly he envisioned himself heading a search party for an escaped convict.

"McGilvrey, you take the basement. O'Hanrahan, you go upstairs. I've got the main floor. Gillespie, stay outside in the car. If you see any funny business, honk twice."

McGilvrey spoke before following the order. "Where do you get off telling us what to do, Colfax? You're not with the department anymore. I thought you worked alone now."

"You thought right, McGilvrey. I don't like giving orders any more than you like taking them. But I owe Police Chief Johnson a favor. When he called to tell me that this kid had escaped jail again, I knew it was payback time."

"Lucky for us," said O'Hanrahan, a tall brooding cop with a sneer on his face.

"No," said Baron, staring down the sneer. "It's lucky for all the citizens in this town who won't have to rely on Emville's finest to make their streets safe again. Now move it, before I get angry."

"If only life was really like that," Baron muttered to himself as he continued to fumble with his one remaining shoelace.

When he finished untying it, he decided that maybe Wilson was right about leaving her shoes on. So he quickly started to tie them up again.

He did not hear the closet door behind him slide open. He felt only the muzzle of a gun press firmly against the back of his neck.

"Freeze," a voice behind him said. "Lie down on the floor with your hands behind your back."

Baron immediately lay facedown on the carpet.

"Hands together."

He took note of the voice. It was young — a child's voice. To be precise, it was the voice of a child trying to sound like an adult. He turned his head so he could speak. "Tucker?"

"No talkin'."

Baron heard a rattling sound. Then he felt a sharp tug on his wrists as Tucker handcuffed first his hands and then his ankles. "Tucker." Baron's tone became less curious and more angry. "Tucker, for cripe's sakes, get me out of these stupid handcuffs."

Tucker was decked out in red and white cowboy boots, blue jeans, a white shirt with a picture of a cowboy on horseback twirling a lasso on the back and a nifty holster. A straw cowboy hat with a whistle hung around his neck. He holstered his plastic pistol and stood up. "I said no talkin', ya mangy varmint. Now where's that woman yer with? She's in a heap a trouble if she thinks she's gonna catch me."

Baron closed his eyes and tried to calm his breathing. This was not how the best detectives went about their business. "Tucker. Let me up, and I'll go get her. We'll play a game together. We'll play cowboys. I love playing cowboys. So does Wilson."

"That her name? Wilson?" Tucker pretended to spit tobacco juice on to the floor. "What kinda handle is that fer a girl?"

"You know what? Let me up and we can both sneak up on her. She can be the good guy and we can be the bad guys. We can rob a bank after. Or even go to the saloon!"

Tucker knelt down so he could look Baron in the eye.

"Y'know what, boy? You talk too much."

"I'll stop as soon as you let me up. I promise."

Tucker removed his pistol and blasted a line of water into the side of Baron's head. "Shut yer yap."

Baron turned the other way and rested.

"Now tell me about this girl yer with." It was Tucker again.

"What about her?"

"She a looker?"

Baron turned to face him. "Pardon me?"

"She got the goods?"

Baron tried to interpret what Tucker was saying. "What are you asking me, Tucker?"

"I'm talkin' about the girl. Wilson. What's she look like? She blond? Brunette? A redhead? She got any curves on her?"

Baron frowned. "How old are you?"

"I'm seven going on twenty-five. How old is she? That's the question."

"Why is a seven-year-old so interested in what a girl looks like?"

"None a yer business. Me and my cousin, Eddie. We hang out a lot. He's told me some things."

"How old is Eddie?"

"Fourteen. He knows a lot."

"Does he dress up like a cowboy?" asked Baron.

"Not no more, he don't. He used to though. All the time."

"What's he told you?"

"You'll find out when Wilson shows up. So will she."

Baron closed his eyes. All he could do was be thankful Wilson was still downstairs. "Tucker?" he said softly. He wanted to negotiate one more time. "Would you mind taking these handcuffs off me?"

"What's it worth to ya?" Tucker asked.

"I'll give you a quarter."

"Forget it. Keep it and buy yourself a gum ball."

"What, did cousin Eddie tell you all about money too?"

"I don't need nobody to tell me what a quarter is. It ain't worth jack." He pretended to spit again. "Now shush. If y'ain't gonna tell me about Wilson, I don't wanna hear yer voice."

"C'mon. A dollar then. It's in my pocket. Please?"

Tucker contemplated Baron's offer.

"Please? Before Wilson gets here?"

Tucker was about to speak when Wilson's voice rang out from the basement. "He's not down here anywhere." He could hear her footsteps on the stairs. "Any luck up there?"

Baron wiggled frantically to free himself.

"C'mon Tucker. Hurry up!"

Tucker ignored him. "I guess I'll find out for myself what she looks like." He ducked back into the closet.

"Tucker!" Baron hissed after him. "Tucker! Let me up!"

Tucker opened the closet door an inch and fired another blast of water at Baron, catching him just below the eye.

"Baron?" He heard Wilson in the kitchen. "Baron?" He could tell by the direction of her voice that she was about to find him. "Bar—? What the...?"

The moment of truth had arrived. There was no daydream that could relieve his embarrassment now or justify his predicament. He couldn't even run into his bedroom and slam the door.

"Baron, what are you doing?" Wilson walked toward him. "Why are you lying on the floor with your hands behind your back?"

He cleared his throat. "No reason."

She crouched beside him. "You found Tucker, obviously."

"I sure did."

"He found you, is more like it."

"Yes."

"So what is he, a cowboy?"

"Among other things."

"He snuck up behind you?"

"While I was tying my shoe."

"Tying it? I thought you were taking your shoes off."

"I was. Then I changed my mind."

"Good work."

"It's your fault." Baron immediately wished he hadn't said that.

"Because I told you to keep your shoes on?"

"Yes." It was too late to take it back.

Wilson shook her head and glanced around the foyer for signs of Tucker. "Boy, I really struck it rich when I hooked up with you two, didn't I?" She looked behind her and saw the closet door silently slide shut. "I mean, between you and Myles, I'm really learning a lot about detective work." She sprang to her feet, grabbed the handle on the closet and held the door closed. "Gotcha!"

Tucker did not respond verbally, but Wilson felt a tug on the door, confirming her suspicions.

"I got him. Tucker, pass me the key to the handcuffs and I'll let you out."

Silence.

"Tucker. Pass me the key."

Still nothing. Then, finally, "Never." His voice was small and shrill.

"Oh, come on. We'll play something else now."

"Come in with yer guns blazin'! That's the only way you'll git me. I'm not comin' out alive!"

Wilson looked dubiously at Baron, who was still lying facedown on the living room carpet. "How did he get those on you? He sounds like he's four years old."

Baron shrugged his shoulders. He didn't feel like talking anymore.

"I'm not four. I'm seven."

Wilson turned back to the mirror. "Why don't you come out so I can see how old you are?"

Tucker's tone of voice changed. "Why don't you come in so I can see how old you are?"

Wilson hesitated. "What?"

"I said why don't you come in? I've got food in here. Plenty to drink."

"You want me to come into the closet?"

"Sure. Why not?"

She looked back at Baron. "Have you actually met this kid?"

He nodded.

"Is he okay?"

He shrugged again.

"What's he talking about?"

"Don't ask him anything," said Tucker from behind the door. "Come in here and talk to me."

Wilson looked momentarily confused.

"He has an older cousin named Eddie who's teaching him about girls." Baron felt the carpet burn his cheek as he spoke. "Apparently they hang out together."

"For real? He told you that?" said Wilson.

"For real," said Baron.

"He's fourteen," said Tucker, obviously aware of what they were saying. "He knows a lot."

"You're learning about girls from your cousin Eddie?" Wilson turned her attention back to Tucker.

"You bet. He has an older brother too, my cousin Tony, who teaches him stuff. Then he tells me."

"Tony and Eddie. Wow. Are you ever lucky."

"You got that right."

"So they're telling you all about how girls and boys are equal and we all deserve the same rights and employment opportunities?"

"What?"

"Is that what your cousin Eddie's telling you about girls?"

"No."

"No? What's he telling you?"

"He doesn't talk about that stuff. He talks about other stuff."

"Oh? Like health issues and what young girls can do to take care of themselves, and how we can make it in a world that is still dominated by men? Is that what he tells you about?"

There was silence for a moment. "No."

"He doesn't talk about that, either?"

"No, he talks about other stuff."

"What other stuff, Tucker?"

"Uhh…"

"Stuff like kissing?"

"Yeah! That stuff."

"He tells you that girls are good kissers?"

"Yeah!"

Wilson shook her head. "Well, you tell your cousin Eddie I'd like to meet him someday."

"Really?"

"Yes, I would."

"I can do that."

"I really wish you would."

"What are your measurements?"

"My what?"

"Your measurements. He says that's the most important thing when you're going on a blind date."

"You tell your cousin Eddie I'd like to see him real
soon in a dark alley where there's no witnesses."

"What's a witness?"

She shook her head. "Forget it."

"Do you still wanna see him?"

"No, I don't."

"Should I give him your number?"

"No, you shouldn't."

"Why not? I bet he might like you."

Wilson chose to ignore him and got back to business.
"So when are you coming out of there? We have a job to
do out here, and I can't do it while my partner's in
handcuffs."

"I have enough food and water in here to last me
three days."

"You do?"

"Uh-huh."

"Wow. What kind of food do you have?"

"None a yer business." Tucker returned to his role as
a cowboy.

Wilson stared at the ceiling and thought for a moment.
Then she smiled. "Tucker, I just thought of something."

"Congratulations. Pick up yer prize on yer way out the door."

"Did you go pee before you started playing this game?"

He hesitated. "What?"

"I said I hope you went pee before you started playing. Even cowboys have to pee, you know."

"I know that."

"Well, I'm just making sure. There's no bathroom in that closet you're hiding in."

"I know."

"So do you want to come out and go pee? You can still be an outlaw. You can pretend to ride a horse and fire your six-shooter."

"My what?"

"Your six-shooter. Haven't you ever heard of one of those?"

"What's a six-shooter?"

"It's the kind of pistol that a real cowboy has. It shoots six bullets, and then you have to load it again."

"Really?"

"Oh yeah. I know a lot about playing cowboys. Me and my sister used to play it all the time." She glanced toward Baron, who seemed to be paying no attention, and carried on her conversation with Tucker.

"You had a six-shooter?"

"A pretend one, but yes. I had a six-shooter. It was very cool."

She felt a slight tug on the door.

"Let me out, please," said Tucker.

"This isn't an ambush, is it?"

"No."

"Are you sure?"

"I have to go pee."

"Promise?"

"Yes. Hurry. I really have to go."

She slid open the door and Tucker walked out.

"Why, you're just a little cowpoke." She looked at him and smiled. He had brown hair and a run of freckles across his nose.

He sneered. "I'm big enough to take him down."

"I can see that."

Baron tried to turn his head.

"Maybe you can undo my partner's handcuffs first. Before you go to the bathroom?"

"Not a chance." Tucker stepped over Baron, popped the whistle from his hat into his mouth and blew as loud as he could as he went down the hall.

"What a sweetie," said Wilson, putting her hands on her hips. "No wonder his mother seemed so homicidal."

Tucker returned a moment later with a key in his hand and the whistle still in his mouth. He continued to blow loudly as he unlocked Baron's hands.

"Thank you." Baron did little circles with his shoulders, wrists and feet to get his blood flowing again.

"How about we go outside now?" said Wilson.

"Deal," said Tucker.

The two of them walked out the front door.

"There's keys on the kitchen table." Wilson called to Baron as they left.

Baron got up off the floor, retied his shoes, retrieved the keys from the kitchen and ran outside to catch up with them.

Baron followed them to a park down the street.

Wilson was pushing Tucker on a swing. She was laughing and chatting with him. He reminded her of some of the kids she used to babysit back in Winnipeg.

Tucker squealed with delight and kicked his feet in the air as she gave him another underduck.

"Higher! Higher!" he shrieked. He leaned over backward and made a funny face at her. She stuck out her tongue and told him to sit up or she'd tickle him.

Baron sat in the swing beside Tucker and scuffed his shoes in the sand. He didn't speak.

He just sat down.

His head hung low.

His shoulders were limp.

He was depressed.

No, he was beyond depressed.

He'd been depressed when he was leaning over his shoes, trying to figure out if he should tie them up or take them off. That's how Tucker had gotten him handcuffed in the first place. He wasn't thinking straight.

Sadness and anger had passed through him about half an hour ago, as he and Wilson walked up the driveway of the Worthinghouse home, mere moments after she'd told him about her rendezvous with Myles.

Embarrassment was long gone. Shocked was old news. Confused left town at the same time the Popsicles were put back in the freezer.

"You wanna take a turn?" Wilson was talking to him.

He didn't care.

What difference did it make if she had anything to say to him now? She'd already declared which one of the two partners she preferred to spend her time with. Why did she care if he wanted to push some horny little brat on a swing? And why should he want to? This was his last job. Who cared if it went poorly?

Besides, how much worse could it get?

"Yo, Mike Hammer. You wanna push Howdy Doody here? It's my turn to sit and do nothing for a change."

He perked up slightly at the name Mike Hammer.

Mike Hammer was one of his favorite detectives — a proud, tough-as-nails creation from the mind of Mickey Spillane, the greatest hard-boiled-crime writer Baron had ever read.

He turned his head so he could see her. "How do you know who Mike Hammer is?"

Wilson shrugged as she gave Tucker another push. "I went to a public school last year in Winnipeg. My English teacher challenged us to read one book every month that was the complete opposite of everything we were interested in. He was such a cool teacher. Detective books were my first pick."

Baron's chest and shoulders slumped even closer to his knees. *No wonder she doesn't like me. We're complete opposites!*

"And you know what? They're still my first pick. I've never read anything so boring in all my life. Although I did read a Louis L'Amour western that was almost as bad. Not quite, but it was very close."

Baron felt his insides stir as she trashed his man Spillane.

"I don't know how anybody can read more than one of those books. I've never been more anxious to get to the last page in my entire life."

If his spirits hadn't been so low, he would have declared such talk fighting words and risen to his feet to defend his prolific hero.

As it was, however, he did nothing.

"What would you read if you had to read a book like that?"

He shook his head. *Now she wants to talk all of a sudden. Last night all she wanted to do was get physical. Not with me, of course. With Myles.*

"I don't know," he said.

"Why not?"

"I've never thought about it before."

"Well, think now. You've got nothing else to do. Apparently you're not on duty anymore."

He ignored the dig and tried to come up with something. What was the opposite of gritty, hard-nosed, blood-on-the-sidewalk detective books? How about girly-girl stories about an annoying little redhead with the goofiest ponytails on earth and a big mouth? "*Pippi Longstocking*," he said.

"There," he muttered to himself. "That's my answer. Now go away."

It was true too. The complete Pippi Longstocking series had sat untouched on Kitty's bookshelf during her entire three years in junior high. Kitty hated reading. When she was little, every time their mom sat down with her to look at a book she would cry and scream.

Nothing made her wail louder than Pippi.

Baron figured the books must be bad if they triggered that kind of a reaction.

Wilson stopped pushing Tucker and put her hands on her hips. "What did you just say?"

Baron, taking note of her reaction, sat up slightly in his swing. "*Pippi Longstocking*. What's wrong with that?"

Wilson came around to the front of the swings where she could look Baron in the eye. Tucker briefly protested, but she ignored him, so he stopped swinging and ran off to the play fort.

Wilson's nostrils flared as she started to speak. "Pippi Longstocking, Mister, is one of the most enlightened, entertaining, self-reliant, free-spirited, breath-of-fresh-air characters in the history of English literature. She makes Anne of Green Gables look like Betty in the *Archie* comics. She makes those chickies in *Little Women* look like pieces of wood."

Baron stared back at her in stunned frightened silence.

"Come on. Defend your position. To say you would not read a *Pippi Longstocking* book means you must know something about them. Otherwise, how would you know you don't like them? Unless you're going to sit there and admit that you have no clue what you're talking about, and you chose her just to shut me up. If that's the case, you're really going to be sorry. I refuse to be treated that way, especially by someone I consider to be my friend."

Baron's confusion returned. Aren't I the one who's supposed to be upset here? he thought. About something more important than a book?

"I'm going to sit here and wait for you to say something." Wilson took over Tucker's swing.

Baron tried to back out of whatever it was he had just gotten himself into. "Maybe I have her mixed up with someone else."

"Impossible. You may not like her, but there is no way on earth you could confuse her with anyone. Unless you're going to tell me that there's someone else out there with superhuman strength and a treasure chest full of gold coins who lives alone in a mansion with a pet horse and a monkey named Mr. Nilsson."

Baron gulped. "It's because of my sister, Kitty. She used to cry whenever Mom made her read. *Pippi* was one of the books she hated most."

"You're kidding me."

"No, I'm not."

"You have to be."

"I'm not."

"How could anyone not like *Pippi*?"

"It wasn't just *Pippi*. She doesn't like reading, period. She never has. That's why she said I shouldn't buy you a book."

"She what?" Wilson's anger was temporarily replaced by curiosity.

"She thought it was a dumb idea. She thinks reading is a dumb idea, except for fashion magazines. She hasn't read a whole book in her entire life."

"Why would you buy me a book? Why would you buy me anything?"

"I didn't. That's what I'm trying to tell you."

"But why would you even think of buying me something? It's not my birthday."

Baron hesitated. He suddenly realized what he had said. "I don't know."

"No, come on. Tell me."

"It was her idea. She thought it would be nice."

"Whose idea? Kitty's? Why would she tell you to buy me something? I don't get it."

Baron couldn't bring himself to tell her the real reason.

Especially not now, with Myles's shadow looming over their heads.

"Was it because of something Myles told you about last night?"

Baron's eyes widened. "Why on earth would I buy you a gift because of last night?" Then he remembered what he'd said about Myles wanting her to become a full-time member of the detective agency.

"Yes," he said, "it had to do with that."

Wilson nodded, as if she had known all along. "So you do know about Pamela then."

"Who?"

"Pamela."

"Who's Pamela?"

"Doesn't that name ring a bell with you? Didn't Myles mention her at lunch?"

"No, he never said anything about a Pamela."

"Are you sure?"

"Of course I'm sure. Why? I thought you said it was just him and you?"

Wilson frowned and shook her head. Something about all of this wasn't adding up.

"So there were three of you, then? You had a party? Invited guests only?" He shook his head as his emotions began to boil again. "Well, all I can say is, I'm glad I listened to Kitty and didn't buy you a book because I'd be taking it back right now. That's exactly what I'd be doing. I'd be taking it right back where I got it from."

Wilson was barely listening to him. Instead she was trying to sort out the events of the past eighteen hours. Specifically, she was trying to determine who knew what, who didn't know what, who was telling the truth and who wasn't.

Then, as the soft, cool spring breeze blew through her hair, she became aware of something else.

She looked around the playground. "Where's Tucker?"

Baron stopped his rant. "Who?"

Wilson whirled around in all directions. "Omigod. He's disappeared."

Baron rose up off his swing and gulped as he scanned the play area.

For the first time all afternoon, he and Wilson agreed on something: Tucker had given them the slip.

CHAPTER FOURTEEN

"Stay calm. Just stay calm and we'll find him."

Baron began to move to the right of the swing set as Wilson moved to the left. There were trees and bushes along two sides of the park. The other two sides opened onto a small field that connected to the sidewalk and nearby streets.

"This is no time to panic. Breathe deep. Keep your eyes open. Keep your ears sharp." In a strange way, he was thankful that such a crisis had presented itself: It gave him a chance to utilize his true skills as a detective, to put into action his experience, knowledge and grace under pressure.

Finally he was the one in charge.

In truth it was the second chance he'd been hoping for.

"Baron." Wilson peered into the fort and found nothing.

"Look for signs. A shoe. His cowboy hat. He can blow his whistle if he's in serious trouble. Just remember to stay calm."

"Baron." Wilson spoke louder this time.

"I say we give it about five, ten minutes tops; then we call his mom. There's no need to panic yet. This type of thing happens all the time. This is a regular occurrence. This is nothing unusual. We'll find him. Don't worry. Panic will do no good for anyone at a time like this."

"Baron, shut up already. We're not calling his mom. He's playing hide-and-seek on us. And stop telling me not to panic. I'll take off my shoe and club you with it if you say that one more time."

Baron stopped his search and stared at Wilson. She was right again. Of course Tucker was playing hide-and-seek. That's what he lived for.

"Did you look over there by the bike rack?" Wilson pointed behind him to the entrance of the park, where a small bicycle rack sat in the grass next to a cluster of tall pine trees.

He remained standing where he was.

In his mind he saw himself as the same private detective he always was — tall and cool, the stub of a cigarette dangling from his lips — standing calmly in the park. He surveyed the grounds around him. He took a pull on his smoke, then flung the butt to the ground and rubbed it out with his shoe. A young police officer, his face so young and fresh Baron felt like pinching his cheek and wishing him a good day at grade school, ran up to his side and began to yap.

Typically, Baron did not like working with the police, but on occasions like this one, where the subject of his investigation was also wanted by the cops, it was unavoidable.

"Where would you like me to go, sir? What would you like me to do? I already checked by the front gate, by the slides and by the concession. There's no sign of the suspect anywhere."

Baron gave him the once-over. "Tell me something, kid."

"Yes, sir?"

"How many times a week do you shave?"

"Excuse me, sir?"

"My guess is twice, whether you need to or not."

"I shave every day, sir. Right after my push-ups and before my shower."

Baron nodded and continued to scan the park. "Push-ups, eh?"

"Yes, sir. I do twenty-five inverted, twenty-five knuckle, twenty-five with my hands together and twenty-five with my hands as far apart as my shoulders. Then I rest for thirty seconds and do them all again with twenty clapping push-ups at the end."

"Attaboy." Baron tapped another cigarette out of his pack. For a joke, he offered one to the young cop.

"Oh no, sir. No, thank you. Not for me."

Baron shrugged, put the package back into the breast pocket of his shirt and noticed for the second time movement in a patch of trees next to the picnic area. "What's your name, officer?" he asked, fishing in his pants pocket for his lighter.

"Sparky, sir."

"Sorry?"

"My name is Johnathon Sparks. But my friends all call me Sparky."

"And I'm your friend already?"

"I'd be honored if you called me Sparky, sir. More than honored, actually. I'd be speechless. I'd be thrilled. My heart —"

Baron caught a glimpse of a face peeking out from behind a thatch of bushes. It was the punk they were looking for. The car and jewelry thief who had thwarted the police so thoroughly that the chief himself had called on Baron for help.

"Listen up, Sparky. Our man is at two o'clock in those bushes by the picnic tables. Don't look. He's watching us. Act nonchalant. Look over there by the bathrooms. Point to the entrance gate and nod like that's where you're going. I'm going to start walking toward him. He's going to make a break for it. When he does, I'll let you know where he's heading."

Constable Sparks took in everything Baron said, nervously pointed to the entry gate and started to slowly walk toward it.

"Walk with authority," said Baron under his breath, but loud enough for Sparks to hear. "Remember, you're a cop."

The thief made his move quickly. He burst out from the bushes and ran straight toward Baron, who calmly stood his ground and curled his fingers into fists. The thief veered sharply toward Sparks.

"Behind you!" shouted Baron, moving with surprising speed and agility. "Take him down!"

Sparks momentarily froze, and then he set himself on a collision course. The thief faked to the right and then cut quickly back to the left. Sparks went with the fake and caught nothing but air, grass and dry dirt with his attempt at a tackle.

The thief caught Baron's right hook in the mug.

"Wow," said Sparks, springing back to his feet, his face red from exertion and embarrassment. "How'd you get here so fast?"

Baron checked his fist for cuts; then he shook it off. "I save my workouts for the battlefield, kid. Now get some support over here. When this punk wakes up, he's gonna be mighty unhappy."

"Hey!" cried Wilson, jarring Baron back to reality. "What was that, another seizure? I said, did you look by the bike rack?"

Baron quickly turned to follow her instruction. What is wrong with me? he chided himself. When am I going to have an idea that's actually a good one? When am I going to get a chance to tell her to do something? When am I going to get it right with her?

"Yoo-whoo! Are you okay?" Wilson was moving closer to him. "Look over by the bike rack; then look in those trees over there. I'm going to look over here."

He felt like saying something. Not like the uncontrolled outburst he'd dumped on her at the office the other night, but something very direct about how he was feeling and what was going on in his mind.

This is not the real me you're talking to, he felt like saying. This is a confused, unsettled, heartbroken version of the real me.

There's a difference!

Four teenagers using the park as a shortcut interrupted him before he could open his mouth.

"Hey, skinny, lose somethin'?" There were three guys — one with a nose that had such a hook you could fish with it, one who was short and fat, another in a green ball cap and sweat pants — and one girl. She was holding hands with the guy in the green ball cap. Baron didn't know which one of them had asked him the question.

"Hey, you got a light?" Green Cap stopped beside him and pulled a pack of cigarettes from the pouch of his hoodie.

"I don't smoke." Baron was startled by their sudden arrival.

"I didn't ask if you smoked. I asked if you had a light."

"And I asked if you lost something," the guy with the nose piped up. "You didn't answer me. What's the matter? English your second language or somethin'?"

Baron could feel his face turning red. He cleared his throat. "I didn't lose anything, no." He did not know why he lied, other than the fact that he didn't want their help, on the off chance that they offered it.

"Did you find him?" Wilson emerged from a patch of trees and walked toward him. "He's not over here, that's for sure."

Baron felt his heart giddy-up into his throat.

The Nose immediately turned and frowned at him. "Why's she asking if you found him if you didn't lose nothing?"

Before anyone else could say anything, Tucker, sitting high in one of the pine trees that Wilson had suggested Baron look in, blew his whistle and shouted very loudly, "Hey, girlfriend, nice jugs!" Then he ducked down in the branches so no one could see him.

Baron nearly died on the spot.

Wilson covered her mouth and closed her eyes.

The girl frowned, blushed and covered herself with her sweater.

The three guys looked around the park.

"Who said that?" said Green Cap.

"I'll kill him," said The Nose.

"No, I'll kill him," said Green Cap. "She's my girl."

"She's my cousin," said The Nose.

"I'm gonna go find him," said the chubby one. He walked toward the pine trees.

Baron gulped. Somebody had to do something before things got out of hand.

"Nobody's gonna kill anybody." It was Wilson again,

coming to the rescue. "It's a little kid playing hide-and-seek in a tree over there. He doesn't mean what he said. No offense." She smiled at the girl as she walked past Baron.

"I'm still gonna kill him." The Nose clenched his fists. "No one talks to my cousin like that."

"Don't blame him," said Wilson. "Blame his cousin, Eddie. He's the one who taught him to think like that. Just carry on where you were going."

"No one's going anywhere until I see this kid," said Green Cap.

"He's up there." Chubs pointed up the tree Tucker was in. "I can see the branches moving."

They all moved to the tree and looked up.

"Get down here, you little puke," said The Nose.

"You got some apologizing to do," said Green Cap.

"Yeah," said Chubs. "You're not supposed to talk to ladies like that. Not even her."

"It's not his fault." Wilson tried again to calm them down. "He's just a kid."

"He's a kid with a big mouth who's gonna be taught a lesson," said Green Cap.

Baron stepped forward and collected himself. He sensed that a different approach was required to get Tucker down from the tree. Fortunately he knew what had to be said and how to say it. "Excuse me, please." He reached his spot and looked up. Way up. "Tucker? Can you hear me?"

No answer.

"Tucker, I'm going to assume you can hear me."

"What does assume mean?" Tucker's little voice sailed clearly down through the branches.

Baron smiled. It was working. "Tucker, can you please apologize so these people can go on their way?"

"What?"

He raised his voice slightly. "I want you to show them the kind of person you are."

"I just did."

"No, I mean the kind of person you really are."

"How do you know who I am?"

"I just do."

"No, you don't."

"I want you to show them the clever and fun and imaginative side of you. Not the smart-mouth side."

It was social-worker talk, straight from his father's mouth. Baron had heard it many times over the years, directed at himself and his siblings, and while it never seemed to work on Kitty, it was effective with Baron and the others.

"You want me to say something?"

"Please." Baron was on a roll. He turned to Wilson and winked. "Be the little gentleman I know you are."

"Okay. Get the girl to come closer to the tree."

Baron and the girl switched places.

"Okay." Baron called up again. "She's ready."

"I'm sorry I said that about your jugs," said Tucker.

The girl covered her mouth and blushed. "I accept your apology," she said back.

"Can you look up here for a second?" Tucker called to her.

"All right." The girl looked up the tree. Tucker sprayed her with his water pistol. "Gotcha!"

She screamed and covered her face.

"I'm going up there." Green Cap threw off his hoodie, pushed Baron to the ground and lunged up the tree. The tall kid started up the tree right beside it. Chubs stayed on the ground with the girl.

"Tucker, get down here!" Wilson called.

Baron closed his eyes and covered his face with his hands.

The two teens were about halfway up their respective trees when Tucker crashed to the ground, using the boughs for support as he came down. He landed with a thud; then he sprang to his feet and dusted off his blue jeans.

Chubs made a grab for him, but Tucker escaped his grasp. Chubs made another attempt but was thwarted by Wilson's kick to his kneecap. He went down in a noisy yelping heap.

Wilson scooped up Tucker and ran through the entrance of the park and down the street. Baron, springing to his feet, quickly followed.

They arrived at the Worthinghouse home several minutes later. Baron fumbled with the key. They got inside and safely upstairs into Tucker's bedroom before the kids, led by Green Cap, appeared on the street. Tucker tried to open his window to shout something, but Wilson covered his mouth until the kids were gone.

At eight o'clock his mom came home.

Baron and Wilson did not receive a bonus, but after privately conferring with her son, Mrs. Worthinghouse did say she would hire them again.

CHAPTER FIFTEEN

In the relative comfort of her cousin's bedroom, Rebecca flopped onto her bed and burst into tears.

She cried for several minutes, then sat up, blew her nose and rose to her feet. Staring straight ahead into the mirror that hung above the chest of drawers, she began to look on the bright side.

It was the way she dealt with things when she didn't feel like talking to her sister.

"I don't have cancer," she said out loud. "Or anything else like it. I'm experiencing no physical pain of any kind. I have a good bicycle. I have a roof over my head." She stopped after each point to sniff and wipe the tears from her eyes. "My mom's getting a portable TV for my bedroom. The plumbing in the house works."

Slowly she began to feel better, as she knew she would.

"I did better than I thought I would on those stupid tests Mom made me write." Then she took a deep breath and began to feel sad again. "I have two friends, sort of. I'm a detective. That's cool."

Her bottom lip began to tremble.

"They both think I'm a complete lunatic." Her hand shook as she wiped a fresh tear from her cheek. "And they're right." The dam broke and she was crying again.

She cried long and loud, but no one heard her because her aunt had taken her mom out to dinner and a movie.

Eventually she stopped and became aware of how quiet the house was. She liked the quiet, but Pamela sure hadn't.

Rebecca remembered that when they were very young, Pamela used to be afraid whenever she woke up in the middle of the night and everything was quiet. They slept in bunk beds in a small bedroom off the kitchen. Pamela was always in the top bunk but when she woke up and everyone else was asleep, she would crawl into bed with Rebecca and the two of them would sleep together until morning. Rebecca never minded sharing her pillows and blankets with her sister — at times like this, she was glad she hadn't minded.

She took several deep breaths until she felt settled enough to go downstairs and make herself a cup of tea.

She washed her face before she went.

She did not want to look distressed or upset in any way when her aunt and her mom returned home. They always asked her too many questions, especially her aunt: What did you do today? Did you go for a bike ride?

Where did you go? Which route did you take? Did you talk to those boys again? When are we going to meet them? What do you mean you keep forgetting to ask them over? What's the matter with you? Have you been crying? Did they say something to you? What's their phone number? Who are they? Why don't we know anything about your life since you came here?

Rebecca had said very little about Baron and Myles, and very soon she wouldn't have to.

Tomorrow, at their regular weekly meeting in the office, she planned on quitting the agency so she wouldn't have to think about them anymore.

Just as importantly, she told herself, they would not have to think about her.

Nothing was making sense to her anymore.

She missed her sister terribly.

She missed her dad. When he wasn't fighting with her mom, he had actually been a pretty decent guy.

She missed her old mom, the one who used to sit and talk with her for hours but who hadn't spent five minutes alone with her since they arrived in Alberta. Not that it was entirely her mom's fault: Auntie Heather was everywhere.

She also missed all her old school friends from the 'Peg, like Shelley Friesen who stayed with her for two weeks after Pamela died, and Margot, Scott, Tammy and Belinda, who attended the funeral and moved to the very front of the church in order to provide her with support so she wouldn't cry when she delivered the eulogy, which she did anyway, but not as much as she might have.

She did not miss her cousin.

She wanted to miss her aunt.

She wasn't sure if she would miss her time at the Blue Whale Detective Agency, but she knew it was time to find out.

CHAPTER SIXTEEN

At the same time that Rebecca was crying on her cousin's bed, Baron was slouched at his desk in his bedroom. With a heavy heart, he wrote his letter of resignation on his computer. It was time to end the daily drama that the detective agency had become.

Wilson, the first love of his life — and quite possibly the last, if the way he was feeling right now was any indication — was gone from his arms forever. It was clear to him now. The fact that she'd never actually been in his arms was irrelevant. He had lost her, fair and square, to his best friend.

The thought of working with the two of them as a couple was too unbearable to even consider.

To whom it may concern, he began. Then he deleted it and started again. He knew darn well to whom his letter concerned. *Dear Myles*, he wrote instead. *Please accept this letter as my resignation from our detective agency*. He hesitated. Should he say "our" or "the" detective agency?

As accurate as "our" was, it sounded too chummy, especially considering the circumstances. But at the same time, maybe he should use "our" as a reminder to Myles of how good things used to be.

He decided to leave it in for the moment, but before he could continue, he was interrupted by Kitty, who walked into his room without knocking and demanded to hear how his date with Wilson had gone.

Baron sighed and turned to face her. He did not really feel like talking, but with her in the room, he knew he would have to.

"Wait. Don't say anything. Let me figure it out." Kitty narrowed her eyes as she studied him. She moved to within a foot of his face and stared as if he were a figure in a wax museum. Then she stood up straight and announced her conclusion. "It sucked."

Baron rolled his eyes. "How'd you guess?"

Kitty smiled and took a seat on his bed. "I'm studying body language at school. It's fascinating."

"You're studying body language at school?"

She nodded. "During math. There's a feature on it in this month's *Cosmo Girl*. I'm awesome at it, already."

He told her about his time with Wilson. "She showed no interest in me at all," he began. "None. She couldn't have cared less what I was wearing. She said no to a Popsicle. I tried everything to start a conversation with her, but all she did was cross her arms and tell me that of course she knew what she was doing because she'd been a babysitter before."

When he got to the part about her private session with Myles in her aunt's backyard, Kitty held up her hand for him to stop. "Tell me you didn't just say what I think you just said."

Baron mournfully nodded his head. "I said it, all right."

"No, you didn't."

"Yes, I did."

"Without photographic evidence, I'll never be able to believe it. Not unless there's another boy named Myles at your school you haven't told me about."

"Ask Wilson. She'll tell you everything she told me."

"What's her phone number?"

Baron shook his head. "I don't mean for real. Just trust me. Why would I make this up? She and Myles got together in her aunt's backyard. He followed her there, so she says. For all I know, she sent him fifteen invitations before he finally accepted one."

Kitty's unblinking eyes remained fixed on her little brother.

"What?" said Baron. "You've heard stories like this before. Maybe not exactly like this, but this is a junior high version of high school, isn't it?"

"Myles followed her to her house?" Kitty was genuinely surprised.

"That's what she said. She could have had him arrested. Instead they got physical."

Kitty's eyes took on a dreamy look. "That is so romantic."

"What?"

"That is so unbelievably romantic. If I didn't have my makeup on, I think I'd start crying."

"Kitty, it's against the law. You can't follow people like that. I mean, we do it all the time when we're on a case, but this is something completely different."

"In all my years of dating I've never once had a guy follow me home."

"That's because you follow them home first. You don't give them a chance to follow you."

"That's not true."

"Sure it is."

"Once, I did that. Okay, two times. Percentage-wise, that's like never."

"Well, he's only done it once too."

"You know, I may be underestimating Myles. His dad's shell-shocked. His mom is a flat-out lunatic. But maybe somehow, like a weed growing through a crack in the sidewalk, he's found a tender romantic side that's starting to blossom."

Baron shook his head again. "I don't think that makes sense. But anyway..." He was through visiting with his sister. "I'm working on something here, so..." He turned his chair around to face his computer.

Kitty stood up. "You're a real trooper if you can get back to schoolwork right after something like this." She began to move toward the door. "I'd be paralyzed for a week if it happened to me. So would the person who did it to me, mind you, but that's another matter."

"I'm not doing schoolwork. I'm writing my letter of resignation from the detective agency."

Kitty stopped. "Are you serious?"

"Hundred percent. More, actually. A hundred and ten percent. And rising."

With unrestrained joy, Kitty rushed over and gave her brother a hug. "My God, Baron. I am so proud of you. I am so — oh, I wish someone would follow me home. That is so cool. But anyway. I am very proud of you."

"Thank you."

"It's time to get out of that stupid shack and get on with your life."

"I agree."

"Take karate or something. Become a man."

"Myles is in karate."

"Go to a different karate school. There's more than one."

"There's only two. He's in one. Rebecca's in the other."

"Then go swimming. Build up your muscles. Rent some time on a tanning bed. I really think you can make something of yourself if you try really, really, really hard."

"I can't go swimming alone. I have epilepsy."

"Then do push-ups. Run around the block. There must be something you can do. Eat red meat."

"I thought that was bad for you."

"You have to cook it first, but Mom can do that. This is so exciting."

Baron turned back to his letter. "You want to hear what I have so far?"

"I can't. I have to go. I'm super late already."

"It's short."

"Baron, sweetie, I have to go. But trust me, anything you say that involves leaving that little shed in the backyard is music to my ears. I am very, very happy for you."

Baron began to feel glum again. "Why don't I feel any of that?"

Kitty gave him a sympathetic smile. "Pain is what we feel in our heart before making the decision that is right and true."

Baron frowned. "Where'd that come from?"

"Ashley Winters and I are writing a song together for graduation."

"Really?"

"We're almost done the first paragraph."

"Songs have paragraphs?"

"Whatever. There's four lines then a space. We're starting to write the second part already."

"What's it called?"

"I just told you. 'Pain is what we feel in our heart before making the decision that is right and true.'"

"That's what it's called?"

"We were going to shorten it, but I convinced Ashley that if we did we'd be selling out."

"How do you even know what 'selling out' is?"

"Candy Bateman's our manager. She read a book

about it. Actually it was an article in a magazine. She read part of it. One of the quotes."

"I didn't know you knew how to write songs."

"There's lots about me you don't know, Baron. You should read my poetry sometime." She stepped into the hallway. "Good luck with your letter. I'll sing you the song when we're finished it."

She left him alone.

Baron began to write again.

CHAPTER SEVENTEEN

At midnight, his weary eyelids barely resisting sleep, Baron had an epiphany, a bright flash of enlightenment that reminded him of all the reasons he had come to love detective work in the first place, and why he was foolish to even think of walking away from it.

Typically, it came to him in a daydream.

"Face it, Baron, your days as a detective are over," said Daphne, the woman at the employment agency. "You have no clients, no money, and from what you just told me, your girlfriend just ran off with your ex-partner to begin a new agency of their own. Now on the bright side, there's a new shoe store opening at the mall next month. They're bound to be hiring. And there's another ad in today's paper for newspaper carriers. Do you have a reliable car?"

Baron ignored the question. He was too depressed to consider selling shoes, but at the same time, he knew he had to make a living somehow.

"I know it's hard to let go of a dream," said Daphne, looking sympathetic. "You know, when I was a little girl, I wanted so badly to be a ballerina. I begged and I pleaded with my parents to sign me up in as many dance classes as I could take, and I practiced every day. In the summer, I'd start every morning with pirouettes on the deck in our backyard. It was such a beautiful time. Then, when I turned sixteen, I—"

"Excuse me," said Baron. "What time is it?"

She checked her watch. "It's ten seventeen."

"What time was my appointment today?"

"Ten o'clock."

Baron smiled at her and rose up from his chair. "Then it took you exactly seventeen minutes to get me off my sorry behind and back in the game again."

"I don't understand."

"Don't ever try to convince someone that it's okay to give up on their dreams. So what if my best friend and business partner just ran off with my girl—if the sun shone every day we'd never know the sweet taste of rain. I'm a detective. That's all I am today and that's all I'll ever be because that's all I want to be. Too bad for you that you didn't get to become a ballerina. Life is too short to quit what you love. Thirty years from now I won't be able to do what I'm doing, even if I'm still here to do it. I'm sorry, lady. I shouldn't have taken up your time. I don't belong here. I belong on the streets, in the alleys. I belong out there where my dream is.

And if you ask me, you do too."

Baron turned to leave. He took two strides and then stopped and whirled around. Daphne had cried out his name as she unpinned the name badge from her blouse and tossed it in the garbage bin. "I was born to dance, and dancing is what I'll do," she said as she threw herself into his arms.

Around them, the rest of the workers at the agency stood and cheered.

The dream made Baron sit up straight in his bed with his eyes wide open and his heart pumping wildly with excitement. The meaning of the dream was clear to him and very simple — detectives don't quit when the heat gets turned up, they get to work. They use their suffering to make them better detectives.

He realized that this was it, right in front of him — his chance to finally become what he had always dreamed of being: a real detective with miseries and sorrows and a past that made him angry and bitter.

"Yes!" he shouted out loud, punching his fist into the air. "Yes!"

He ran into Myles the next morning at school.

"Hey," he said. He was feeling tough. Not sick-tough, like with a cold or a headache, but tough-tough, like the detectives he admired. The guys who would never, ever give up.

"Hey," said Myles. "How'd it go yesterday at Tucker's house?"

"Peachy."

"Peachy?" said Myles.

"Best case I've ever been on."

"Really?" said Myles. "How was Wilson?"

"She was great. Awesome. I'm looking forward to working with the two of you for a long, long time." He smiled. "For ever and ever, till death do us part."

Myles gave him a curious look. "Are you okay?"

"Never been better. Why?"

"You're acting weird."

"Am I?"

"Yeah. Really weird."

"I'd say I'm acting like a guy who's just discovered something."

"Oh yeah?"

"You bet."

"And what is that?"

Baron started to very slowly nod his head. Then he started to shake it back and forth. Then he stopped and started nodding again. "I'll save it until tonight."

"Why?" said Myles.

"Because I want to."

"Then Wilson'll hear it."

"So be it," said Baron, with a shrug. "You'd probably tell her anyway, right? Over ice cream at her house or a glass of Moira's iced tea at the coffee shop?"

Again, Myles looked at Baron as if the two boys had never met before. "Are you sure you didn't fall on your head yesterday?"

"I'm sure you wish I had."

"What?"

"I'm sure you two probably wish for a lot of things, starting with me submitting my letter of resignation so the two of you can work together without interruption."

Myles studied his friend's face for a clue to his behavior. "Baron, what are you talking about?"

"I think you know," said Baron.

"You think I know what?"

"Exactly what you just said."

"What did I just say?"

"You asked me what I was talking about."

"Okay."

"And I think you know what I've been talking about."

"Why would I ask what have you been talking about if I knew what you've been talking about?"

"Because you don't want to admit it."

"Admit what?"

"You know."

Myles hesitated, and then he shook his head and began to make his way to his next class. "We'll talk about this later," he said as he left.

"See?" said Baron, with a final nod. "I knew you knew."

At the meeting, before Wilson could hand in her letter of resignation, Baron cleared the air, still feeling that he was living out a dream. "First of all, just let me say congratulations to you both. You make a lovely couple. I wish you the very best. The bad news is, I ain't goin' nowhere. Not today. Not tomorrow. Not any day in the foreseeable future. I'm staying right here and I'm going to do the work that I love most, and if I work alone, fine. If I work with a partner, that's fine too. But I'm going to do detective work. It's in my blood. It's who I am, and I'm not about to quit being myself."

He stood up and started to pace around the shed. "But I'll tell you something. I came this close to packing it all in last night. This close." He held his thumb and forefinger a hair's breadth apart. "I was ready to say forget it. They're in love. They don't want me around. Leave them alone and go find something else to do with your life, which led naturally to the question, what? What else would I do? What else is there to do? I came up with exactly nothing. Not one thing. This is it for me, people. So I had to make a decision: Do I stay on, and make life uncomfortable for everyone here, or do I move on? Ironically the answer came to me from my sister. Earlier in the evening, when I was convinced that I had no option but to leave, she had said to me, 'Baron, pain is what we feel in our heart before making the decision that is right and true.' That is what I'm doing now. I'm making a decision that is right and true, and it is causing me pain. But I have to do it. I have to."

He sat down. "I have to." He shook his head. "I just —"

"May I interrupt?" It was Wilson.

"Please do," said Myles.

"If it's about talking me out of my decision, don't bother," said Baron, staring at the floor. "Nothing you say will make me change my mind. Nothing."

"It's not about that," said Wilson. She had a small white envelope sitting on her lap.

"No tricks, either," said Baron. "I'm firm on this. I may be the only one here who doesn't know karate, but I'll go to the mat with anyone to defend myself."

Wilson, who had been about to submit her own resignation, abruptly changed course.

"You'll what?" she asked.

"I'll go to the mat with either of you," repeated Baron, raising his eyes to hers to confirm just how serious he was.

"What does that mean?"

"It means he's ready to fight," said Myles. "It's an expression we use. Not very often, obviously."

"You want to fight me?" said Wilson.

Baron explained himself. "I'm not saying I want to. I'm saying I will."

"You will fight me?" said Wilson.

"Yes, if I have to."

Wilson shook her head, took in a deep breath of air

and let it out slowly. "Wow," she said out loud but to herself. "And I thought I was crazy."

"I'm not crazy," said Baron. "I'm serious. You two can run off and do whatever you want. I'm not leaving. That's all I'm saying. Last night I was ready to. I wrote a letter and everything. Then I realized that this right now is the very point I've been working toward my entire reading life. I daydream all the time about being a detective. About being a tough guy and a cool guy. This is my passion. This is where I live. And as of this very moment, this is who I am."

"Now you're starting to freak me out," said Wilson.

"Me too," said Myles.

"We have to sort this out because there is something really wrong here," said Wilson. "Myles follows me to my house and listens to me talk to my dead sister. Then for some reason he tells you he wants me to become a permanent member of the agency, and out of all that, all you have to say is some jibber-jabber about your daydreams and where you live?"

There was silence in the office for a moment.

"You told her that I wanted her to become a permanent member of the agency?" said Myles.

"You have a dead sister?" said Baron.

"You didn't say anything to him about the other night?" said Wilson.

"Yes, I did," said Baron to Myles.

"Yes, I do," said Wilson to Baron.

"No, I didn't," said Myles to Wilson.

"Well, I'm right then," said Wilson. "We have some straightening out to do. I'll start."

For the next two hours there were tears, laughter, denials, apologies, much repeating of information and one seizure. The meeting ended just before ten. The Blue Whale Detetctive Agency was still intact, and Wilson had been officially invited, and subsequently welcomed, as its newest permanent member.

When Baron lay down in bed later that night, his hands behind his head on the pillow, he enjoyed a daydream that was quite different from his usual ones: This one involved someone he actually knew.

"So how does this work, exactly?"

It was Kitty, standing in the doorway of the office.

He hesitated before answering. Kitty had never visited him here before. "Sorry?"

"I come in. I sit down. I tell all. You go catch the bad guy. Is that pretty much it?"

He closed his eyes and rubbed his forehead, the way people do when they feel a headache coming on. "Why do you ask?"

Kitty entered the office, sat down and smiled at him. Actually, she glowed. "Did you say why?"

"Yes, I did."

"As in, why are you expressing such interest in my

work as a detective after years of writing me off as a loser?"

"Sure."

Kitty leaned forward. Her eyes grew large. "I'm writing a movie."

Baron frowned. "I thought you were writing a song."

"It's grown into a musical…What can I say? The song got to be ten pages long, and Ashley and I still weren't finished it so we thought, We have more to say than we thought we did. We should do a whole album. Then Candy, our manager, said, 'No, wait. You should do a musical because then I could dance in it.' So here I am. I'm writing a musical. Isn't that awesome?"

Baron took a moment to think. "I guess so."

"You guess so? Baron, do you know how much blood, sweat and tears it takes to write an entire movie? And this isn't going to be full of clichés either. This is going to be a real story."

"What's it about?"

"We don't know that yet. We have to workshop it."

"You have to what?"

"I don't know. Candy's been reading something again. I don't understand it."

"Well, good for you." Baron looked down at the case he'd been reviewing before Kitty's arrival. "Thanks for coming all the way out here to tell me about it. Is there anything else? I've got a ton of work to do."

"Of course there's something else."

"What is it?"

"I need you to tell me all about being a detective. See, I even brought a notepad." She pulled a tiny notepad from her hip pocket, with a tiny pencil attached to it.

"Why?" said Baron.

"Because it's very important for me to know."

"How come?"

"So the character I'm working on in my movie is believable."

"I don't get it."

"Baron...*hello*. I'm writing a movie. It's going to be a blockbuster. There has to be crime in it. Good guys. Bad guys. Cops on the take. People getting killed. A young beautiful female officer who seduces two different cops and no one knows until the end if she's going to be the killer or the one who saves everyone."

"I thought you said this was a musical?"

"I did say it was a musical."

"It doesn't sound like a musical."

"That's because you haven't heard the music yet. How can you say it doesn't sound like a musical if you haven't even heard the music? God. Everyone's a critic all of a sudden. This is so difficult."

Baron shook his head. "Okay. So what do you want to know?"

Kitty leaned back in her chair and prepared to write. "Okay. First, what drawer do you keep your whiskey in?"

"I don't drink, Kitty."

She smiled at him and winked. "Come on, Baron. I know you're a sweet boy. But we all have our dark sides. Where is it?"

"Kitty, I don't have a drawer in this office. Look around you. There's no desk. There's this crummy little round table and a few chairs."

Kitty wrote in her notepad. "Okay, where's the sexy secretary?"

Baron shook his head.

"Every detective on every TV show or movie that I've ever seen has a sexy secretary." Kitty looked around the office. "So where is she? Where's she hiding?"

"Kitty," said Baron.

"I'm not leaving until I find her."

Baron sighed. Then he started to think. As a detective, he'd managed to get out of every tight spot he'd ever been in. It's what made him as good as he was, and he was very, very good. "She's gone home for the evening," he said.

"For real?"

"You just missed her."

"What's her name?"

"Trixie. I hired her after I busted her old man. Some little punk grifter who was shaking down old ladies on their way home from the grocery store. She was the one who tipped me off. She wanted to get away from him, but he wouldn't let her leave."

"What do you mean you busted him? What did you do?"

"I fed him a double serving of knuckle pie, that's what I did. Then the cops came, scraped him off the sidewalk and threw him in the slammer."

"You fought him?"

"I wouldn't call it a fight. More like target practice with my fists. I got nothin' but bull's-eyes."

"Are you serious?"

"Of course I'm serious."

"Omigod."

"Reminded me of the time a pair of toughs from the city came out here to hustle one of my clients for money they claimed she owed them. I happened to be with her at the time, reviewing some notes on the case I was working on. I asked them nicely to leave, once. Not-so-nicely a second time. Then one of them got upset and took a poke at me. I think he ended up getting out of the hospital a week earlier than his friend who came at me with a shovel. They both needed surgery."

Kitty stared at her brother in silence. She hadn't written a word of his story down.

"You gonna document any of this, or should I just call you the next time there's trouble?"

Kitty's mouth hung open. She was speechless.

"I could fill that little notepad of yours in an hour with stuff like this if you want me to. I don't know how you're gonna put it to song though."

"I never knew this was what you did back here."

"None of it happens right here, kid. The action's out there on the street, in the alleys, on rooftops."

"You've fought on a rooftop?"

"Once, I did, yes."

"What if you fell off?"

"When I get hired to do a job, I do the job. If it means chasing some pussycat up a tree and onto a roof, I chase him up the tree and onto the roof. In this particular case, once we got up there he decided he wanted to fight. So we fought. He was twice my size, half my speed, and ten times dumber than a sack of doorknobs. He fell off after I socked him one in the jaw. I waited for the ladder."

"Baron, you are incredible," said Kitty, her eyes wide.

"I'm still your little brother," he said modestly.

"I have to tell Ashley about this. She is going to die. She will absolutely die."

"I hope she has a will. Greedy relatives make up half my caseload."

"I'll ask her," said Kitty, rising quickly to leave. "Omigod, this musical is going to be so amazing."

She left on the fly.

Baron shook his head and went back to reviewing his case.

When he woke up the next morning, he grinned as he remembered his dream. He really wouldn't put it past Kitty to write a musical.

Then he remembered his other dream, the real one about becoming the detective that he always wanted to be and not letting anything or anyone get in the way of it, and he smiled the way the cool Baron in his dreams always smiled.

For the first time ever, he actually felt like himself.